drama queen

aly welch

WRITING BLOC
INDIE PUBLISHING TEAM

I dedicate Drama Queen to all the talented cast and crew I've had the privilege of knowing who understand the importance of camaraderie on stage and behind the scenes.

one

. . .

Caitlyn Smith barely made it into the subway car before the 2 left the station. To her relief, she found an empty seat and collapsed into a tired, sweaty heap. Her long light brown hair, limp from an afternoon of running all over the theater district and dancing her proverbial tail off, fell out of a loose bun and into her face as she leaned back in her seat and closed her eyes.

Caitlyn gnawed on the inside of her lip, worried. Her last several auditions had gone poorly, and she knew her roommates were growing frustrated with her late and sometimes incomplete contributions to the rent. She barely noticed when someone sat down next to her until they tapped on her shoulder.

Against her better judgment, Caitlyn removed her earbuds and turned to her right. She saw an older man in the seat beside her. Wearing a stained, rumpled suit, he had frizzy gray hair and wild eyes.

He hissed in her ear. "They're everywhere, you know. The Fae. They could be your next-door neighbors, and you'd never be the wiser. I tried to tell my superiors, but they wouldn't listen. Said I'd been on the job too long, that maybe I needed a break. You'd think the people in power, that they'd know about these things, but they haven't got a clue." He chuckled to himself. "No, sir. They don't know shit. But you and me, we're smarter than them. We won't let the others get the jump on us."

Caitlyn forced a smile that looked more like a grimace. "No, sir," she agreed.

Why do the nutty ones always sit by me?

At least his pants were fully buttoned. Apart from tapping on her shoulder, he had kept his hands to himself—so probably not a creeper, just crazed. If Caitlyn's father knew some of the things she encountered in New York City—which, in all honesty, weren't much worse than some things people pretended never happened in Ohio— he'd cut her off and insist she move back to their suburban home near Cleveland. But she wasn't ready to give up on her Broadway hopes and dreams.

Not just yet.

Especially not today. Caitlyn couldn't wait to tell her roommates about her new opportunity. She'd gotten the message after her last audition, which had gone so poorly that running home to her father hadn't sounded so bad.

Caitlyn blinked, realizing the strange man no longer sat beside her. Instead, he'd moved on to somebody else several seats away. A middle-aged, scholarly-looking man in a sweater vest with wire-framed glasses caught Caitlyn's eye and chuckled. "I've never seen someone carry on an entire conversation with themselves without talking aloud before, but it sure scared that whack job off. Good show. I'll have to try it myself the next time I have unwanted company."

Another grimace. "Thanks?"

She put her earbuds back in and looked down at her phone. A genuine smile spread across Caitlyn's face as she re-read the message. She'd been invited to audition for workshopping a prospective musical by an up-and-coming playwright and director. The son of a former Broadway producer and a moderately successful soprano, Elliot Dunn was considered brilliant by all accounts. His play about a homeless man turned hero called *A Knight in Brooklyn* was a commercial hit off Broadway, with favorable reviews apart from the occasional criticism of being derivative of some 1980s movie.

Caitlyn never saw it because, well, it sounded like a bit of a downer, and even off-Broadway productions weren't exactly in her budget. But it must have been good if it helped him attract enough investors to secure a venue and hire performers and crew for a workshop. A steady paycheck was good. A chance at making a Broadway show?

An absolute dream come true!

Caitlyn closed the email. She opened her calendar to input her audition time and gasped.

Rent was due.

Rent was due, and Caitlyn was short a couple hundred bucks. Dominique was going to kill her. Or at least sigh heavily and roll her eyes at their other roommates, Naomi and Harper. Caitlyn cringed at the thought of calling her father for help, again, and on such short notice, but dialed anyway. He didn't answer.

"Hey, Dad? It's me, hey look, I'm sorry to ask for help again, but I'm $200 short on rent. Good news, though. I'm auditioning for a workshopping gig tomorrow. It's basically like a steady job, I mean, as long as I don't get cut during the process or whatever. I'm sure it'll be great. I mean, I still have to get the par—"

Click.

"—rt."

Caitlyn shrugged. He'd get the idea.

Caitlyn shared a small two-bedroom apartment in Brooklyn with three other young women, all in their early twenties. Dominique was a legal assistant, and Naomi and Harper worked in accounting. Twenty-year-old Broadway hopeful Caitlyn was the odd one out in more ways than one.

When Caitlyn walked in, Dominique looked up from one of the mismatched chairs in what passed for their living room. She still wore a blazer, blouse, and pencil skirt, but her heels were on the floor. Even after a long day at work, Dominique looked striking with her short auburn hair, high cheekbones, and smooth brown skin—a far cry from the hot mess that was a blotchy disheveled Caitlyn in her oversized hoodie, faded black leggings, and scuffed ballet flats.

"Did you contact that staffing agency I gave you the card for?" Dominique peered at Caitlyn's face, her brown eyes tired but inquisitive.

Caitlyn made a face. "Yeah, but they needed open availability. It's just not a good fit with my schedule." She noted the way Dominique's lips twitched in annoyance. "But I have a lead on a steady job."

Dominique's face relaxed into a smile. "That's great. I—"

"I still have to audition," Caitlyn continued, "but the pay for workshopping isn't bad, and if they like me enough, I'll finally land my first Broadway gig."

Dominique's smile faded. "I see. You have your share of the rent for me, though, right?"

Caitlyn bit her lip before speaking. "Just about. Some crazy person accosted me on the subway and I forgot to call Dad until I was almost home. I left him a message to ask if he can help fill in a teeny gap for me, so he should be moving money into my account at any minute now." Caitlyn looked down at her phone. "Any minute…"

One of the bedroom doors opened. Naomi, wrapped in a towel, poked her head out. "Did Caitlyn give you her portion of the rent yet?" She glanced at Caitlyn. "Oh hi, Cate." She grinned, her full lips a deep vibrant red instead of the more neutral shade she wore at work and her ebony hair falling over her shoulders in soft waves. Getting ready for a date, Caitlyn presumed. Harper had a steady boyfriend, too. Caitlyn couldn't remember the last time the diminutive blue-eyed blonde had slept in the room they shared.

"Cate has assured me that our fifth roommate will be taking care of things," Dominique told Naomi with a wry grin. "As per the usual."

"Ooh," Naomi purred. "*He's* my favorite. He never leaves wet towels on the floor or finishes the milk without replacing it." She arched an elegant brow at Caitlyn, her brown kohl-lined eyes sparkling with amusement, before she slipped back into the room she shared with Dominique.

Caitlyn's ears burned. She looked at Dominique, but the other woman was busy typing something on her phone, looking strained and unhappy. Caitlyn sighed and retreated to the room she shared with Harper.

Harper's side of the room was neat and tidy, with photos of family and friends in jeweled frames on her elegant wooden dresser. She had a matching wardrobe, and her bed was always made, though she hadn't slept in it for the last few nights.

Caitlyn did not have enough belongings to call her side of the room messy, but her bed was never made, and her rainbow leopard print blanket had fallen halfway on the floor. She had so few clothes she lived out of a duffle bag, favoring light stretchy fabrics that weren't prone to wrinkling. A heavy winter jacket and lightweight windbreaker hung from hooks on a flimsy coat rack she'd found on the sidewalk months ago. She removed her faded hoodie and added it to an available hook before laying down on her bed. Her pillow was so worn, it contained three distinct clumps of stuffing. Caitlyn patted it into shape before slipping it behind her head.

Her phone rang. Caitlyn pushed herself back up, crossing her legs as she answered. "Hi, Dad."

"This is the third time in as many months you've asked for extra money," Kurt Smith said. "Honey, I don't think this is working out."

"I know, Dad, and I'm sorry, but things are looking up, I swear. I have a really big opportunity tomorrow, and if all goes well, money won't be a problem again. Not for a long time, maybe not ever."

"Try to temper your expectations," her father advised. "I'm moving money over, but if this audition doesn't work out, I think it's time we have a serious talk. If nothing else, you should look into a cheaper rental situation. Maybe double or triple up on a studio apartment if you have to. I know you don't do much more than sleep in your place, anyway."

"Thanks, Dad, but Dominique's been really good to me. I'd hate to leave her hanging. I should probably get some rest. Been a long day. I have to get up early tomorrow."

"Love you," her father said.

"Love you, too."

Caitlyn put down her phone and glanced at the only two pictures she had, both in light-weight frames affixed to the wall with putty.

One was of Caitlyn and her father after her high school graduation. Kurt Smith had a receding hairline, brown eyes, and a kind smile. He stood next to Caitlyn, wearing a button-down shirt and slacks, his work attire sans the sport coat. She wore an old floral dress of her mother's, a little old-fashioned maybe, but Caitlyn liked to think of it as vintage.

The other picture was taken at Caitlyn's thirteenth birthday party, a year before her mother, Catherine, died from ovarian cancer. The wispy remains of Catherine's once thick brown hair were concealed under a scarf, but she beamed at the camera, her hazel eyes sparkling.

Caitlyn wiped a few tears from her cheeks and laid back down. She didn't hear Dominique knock on the door or push it open ten minutes later, nor did she notice Dominique cover her with her blanket and turn off the light before closing the door again.

———

"We need to talk," Dominique said to Caitlyn as she handed her a granola bar the next morning. "I didn't get a chance to tell you last night, and I know you have to leave soon, so I'm just going to come out and say it. I put out an ad for roommates. I've already scheduled some interviews. A couple said they can move in as soon as today if we decide they're a good fit."

"Oh. Is Harper moving in with her boyfriend?"

"Also," Dominique said, fixing Caitlyn with a meaningful stare.

"Is Naomi moving in with Harper's boyfriend, too?"

"Catie…"

"Is this about the rent? Because Dad put the money in my account. I can send it to you right now." Caitlyn pulled her phone from her hoodie.

"It's about a lot of things." Dominique sighed. "You're a very sweet girl, but Naomi and I have been talking, and we just don't feel like this is the right place for you." The way she said it, it almost sounded like she meant more than just the apartment.

"But what am I supposed to do?" Caitlyn blinked back tears, finding it hard to work her jaw to speak as her lips trembled. "I have nowhere else to go."

"Do you want my honest opinion? As a friend?" Dominique squeezed Caitlyn's shoulder.

Caitlyn nodded.

"Go home."

Though Dominique's voice was kind, the words felt like a punch in Caitlyn's gut. Her eyes widened as she stared into Dominique's somber face.

"I've seen what this place does to girls like you. What it's already doing." She tucked a loose strand of hair behind Caitlyn's ear. "Go back home where you can be a big fish in a small pond instead of…I dunno, one of the feeders in a shark tank. Maybe in a few years, when you have more experience and some actual savings, you can give it another try."

Caitlyn turned away and returned to her room, blinking back tears. She took her jackets off their hooks and forced them into her bag, along with her boots. Sighing, Caitlyn realized she had no room for her bedding, but as of now, she didn't have a bed anymore either— that had come with the room—so it didn't seem to matter. The last thing she did was remove her photos from the wall and slip those into the top of her duffle bag.

"I didn't mean you had to leave first thing," Dominique said when Caitlyn came back out. "If you need a day or two to sort things out, we can work with it."

"Whatever. It's fine." Caitlyn steeled herself as she walked past. "I gotta go."

Hoisting her overstuffed bag, Caitlyn shuffled down the sidewalk. The first rays of sunlight were only beginning to touch the velvety dark blue sky. She pushed aside her dismay over losing her room to focus on her audition. In the back of her mind, she knew it might be her last chance in this town, but she couldn't let the pressure get to her or she'd blow it for sure.

An animal scurried past her on the sidewalk, too big for a rat but smaller than a cat.

Squirrel maybe?

"Hey, baby, lemme help you with that," someone said, a hoodie obscuring his face as he stepped in front of Caitlyn.

"Nah, I got it." Caitlyn glared as he stepped closer. "I am *not* having a good morning, so why don't we pretend I've already kicked you or whatever so we can both move on with our li…" She trailed off as the man stared at something behind her, his hood falling back to reveal a scruffy face and wide, bloodshot eyes. He fled.

Caitlyn turned to look at what had startled him, but all she saw was the tail of some dark furry animal disappearing into an alleyway. A different animal from before—unless it had one hell of a growth spurt.

"Huh. Thanks for the assist."

Caitlyn shrugged and kept walking until she reached the entrance of the subway station.

two

. . .

As soon as Caitlyn sat down, she pulled her phone out of her hoodie to look up the address for the morning's audition again. The Blackstone Theater was in Hell's Kitchen. It sat four hundred and eighty people. She had performed there once before, her first named role as a character in *A Chorus Line*, a departure from the edgier fare the venue favored. She played one of the dancers, cut at the top of the show, but she was an understudy to three of the supporting actresses—none of whom missed a performance during the show's brief run.

When the Q arrived in Hell's Kitchen thirty minutes later, Caitlyn huffed as she lifted her bag and got out of the train. Fortunately, the Blackstone Theater was only a couple of blocks away. Her stomach growled as she smelled bacon cooking in a diner on the way to the theater. Maybe she'd treat herself to a real breakfast if her audition went well.

The front of the house was closed, so she walked around the theater to a door in the back, which had been propped open. The dimly lit hall was lined with dressing rooms, a couple bathrooms, and an office. A light flickered as she walked down the hall. Caitlyn looked up at the ceiling and bumped into someone with her massive duffle bag.

"Woah, what'd you do, bring your entire wardrobe? I don't think you'll have time for any costume changes during your audition." The speaker stood at Caitlyn's height. He had unruly brown hair, brown eyes, and a wry grin.

"I got kicked out of my apartment," Caitlyn blurted out, breathless. She dropped her duffle bag at her feet.

The man ran his fingers through his hair, mussing it even more. "Wow, sorry to hear that." His eyes narrowed. "Hey, don't I know you?"

Caitlyn shrugged. "I was in *A Chorus Line* last fall. I'm Caitlyn." She took a closer look at him. He did not appear to be much older than she was, and she recognized the smirk. "You're one of the sound guys, right? Uhm, Tim…Tom?"

"Tyler."

"I was close! I had the first letter right, anyway," Caitlyn said, grinning. Someone began vocalizing onstage. A high soprano from the sound of it. Caitlyn reached for her bag. "I should go warm up, too. I haven't even stretched yet."

"You should probably leave your stuff in the back." Tyler reached for her bag and winced as he picked it up. "I…promise…to keep it safe. Not like they'll be needing me for any sound effects."

"Thanks!" Caitlyn's grin widened. She may have been homeless, but she'd made a new friend. That had to count for something. Right?

———

Tyler rolled his shoulder a few times as he walked down the steps on the side of the stage. His roommate, Max, caught up with him in the aisle on the way back to the control booth. He was tall and lanky, with a dark brown buzz cut and piercing blue eyes. He wore a plaid flannel shirt, baggy jeans, and a headset. His voice sounded tense as he said, "Hey man, thanks for coming in to keep me company today."

"No problem. I hate manning the booth alone. Gives me the creeps."

"That's not what I—"

"Kidding." Tyler laughed. "Elliot puts me on edge, too."

Max opened the door to the control booth and flicked on the lights. "I know he's paying Manny good money to rent the place, and he seems nice enough, but there's something about him. I dunno."

"I think it's the nepotism," Tyler said. "As working-class craftsmen, we're predisposed to hate him."

Max laughed. "Yeah. The guy has one critically acclaimed off-Broadway show under his belt, and now people are trusting him to develop a Broadway musical? Based on *Dracula*?" Max narrowed his eyes. "Hasn't that been done?"

"Once," Tyler said, "but it was a big flop. Sounds like Elliot Dunn pitched the investors something more artistic and less…hokey, I guess. Full orchestra, no synthesizers or electric guitars. And he's ditching the love story between Dracula and Mina, restoring the horror of the original novel, blah blah blah." He waved his hand as he spoke.

"I dunno," Max said. "Still sounds like schlocky shit to me."

"Schlock sells." Tyler shrugged. His eyes fell on Caitlyn as she talked to some of the other women auditioning first thing this morning. Six women were scheduled per hour block for the next several hours. He knew the leading role of Mina had already been cast, but her best friend, three vampire brides, and half a dozen choral parts were up for grabs.

"On it," Max told someone on his headset. He brought up a light center stage.

Caitlyn stepped into it. She nodded to the piano player on the side of the stage. Tyler recognized the opening bars of "Wishing You Were Somehow Here Again" from *The Phantom of the Opera*. Not the most original choice, but that minor criticism was forgotten when Caitlyn began to sing.

"Not bad," Max said when she finished. "That break at the end was actually a nice touch. Just enough to show some emotion."

"I think that was legit. She got kicked out of her apartment."

Max turned to Tyler. "You know her?"

"Sort of. Her name's Caitlyn. She was in *A Chorus Line*. Do you remember?" Tyler slapped his hand against his forehead. "I told her I'd watch her stuff. Then I helped Manny replace a light and forgot all about it. I'm sure it's fine, but I should probably run back down to check so she doesn't freak out."

Max wasn't paying attention. Instead, he stared at the next performer onstage, aghast.

"Is that a Tiffany Sharp song?"

———

"I thought about doing something from *Phantom*, but everybody does." The statuesque blonde tossed her braid over her shoulder as she addressed the group. "You sounded good, though," she told Caitlyn. "I'm sure they'll overlook that bum note near the end."

She exchanged a smirk with her friends, one tall and pale with dark brown hair, the other short with a smattering of freckles across her nose and lighter brown hair. Caitlyn remembered Anne Marie Sloane and her friends Sophia Gibson and Elise Major as leads in *A Chorus Line*. She hadn't liked them much.

"I thought you sounded amazing," a soft voice said.

But Caitlyn had already turned to someone else to ask, "Is this your first audition? I don't think I've seen you before."

"Maya Jackson," the other woman said. She had glossy black hair, golden brown skin, and hazel eyes that sparkled when she turned to Caitlyn, grinning. "I just finished touring as the understudy for Eponine."

"Oh, wow. I've always wanted to do *Les Mis*."

"The main Eponine was out sick a lot, and I even opened in a few towns to favorable reviews. I guess that's why Elliot Dunn called me personally to audition." Maya walked away and began to stretch.

"I'm surprised she even has to audition."

Now Caitlyn turned to look at Laurel Locke. Laurel was small and thin with pale blond hair and big brown eyes. She didn't have the strongest voice, but she came alive when she danced. The rest of the time she almost seemed to fade into her surroundings. Honestly, not the worst strategy in this town. Caitlyn liked her. She gave her a wry grin and said, "I should've told Anne Marie her reinterpretation of that Tiffany Sharp song sounded like something you'd hear on reality TV."

Laurel furrowed her brow but nodded.

Max was staring up at the ceiling when Tyler returned from checking on Caitlyn's bag, which was still safe and sound at the end of the hallway. "I could swear I heard something scurrying around up there."

"Probably just rats. I thought Elliot was the only critter giving you the creeps."

Max rolled his eyes at Tyler. "Whatever. All I know is he better get somebody else to work the spotlight if this mess ever sees an audience because I don't want to get stuck up there. It somehow manages to be claustrophobic and drafty all at the same time. Blech."

"You know, it's probably going to end up being you and me on light and sound, and he'll get one of the newbies to do it." Tyler sat down next to Max, and they watched the choreographer teach the auditioners a short dance routine.

Max snorted when Anne Marie stumbled on stage. "I hope Elliot doesn't cast her and her friends. They remind me of the mean girls I went to school with. Stirred up so much drama during that run of *A Chorus Line*, even by theater standards."

"Do you miss it?" Tyler asked after a beat.

"School?"

"No, performing."

Max shook his head. "Not even a little." He pushed the play button and turned up the volume as the women on stage danced in time to the music. "I'm happier being myself."

Isabella Moreno did not mess around. Only thirty-two bars of music, and her choreography had Caitlyn sweating. Even Anne Marie looked ready to fall over, with her normally sleek blond hair slipping out of her braid and falling around her flushed face in a tangled mess. It was the sort of contemporary dance that Laurel specialized in, but Isabella had promised—or threatened, depending on one's perspective— everything from lyrical to ballroom dance, even hip-hop. Caitlyn didn't know how well hip-hop would lend itself to Victorian England, but she was open-minded.

"Thank you," Isabella said after they finished leaping and swirling to eerie music that built to a threatening crescendo as they threw themselves to the floor. Though her dark auburn hair was pulled back into a severe bun, the choreographer's smile was warm and genuine. Some of them, perhaps all of them, pleased her.

Elliot Dunn was harder to read, his blue eyes cool behind elegant wire-framed glasses. He had curly, dirty blond hair, and a pen tucked behind his ear—when he wasn't scribbling notes onto a pad of paper. Beside him sat one of the most beautiful women Caitlyn had ever seen. Her dark hair and eyes contrasted with her pale skin, but she looked luminous rather than sickly. Caitlyn hadn't been surprised when Elliot introduced Leanne Snow as his Mina, even though she'd never heard of her before.

"Yes, thank you all for auditioning. You'll hear from us by Wednesday if you're called back," said Carol Johansson, one of the show's producers. Everything about the older woman screamed money, from her polished blonde bob to her elegant suit. The auditioners nodded and turned to leave.

"Think I should go red?" Anne Marie asked her friends, holding a strand of her own blonde hair as they walked offstage.

Caitlyn rolled her eyes at Anne Marie's back, then paused. She looked back over her shoulder. She could swear Elliot was watching her, but it was hard to tell the way his glasses now reflected the house lights.

Hope that's a good sign.

three

. . .

"You did great." Tyler stood beside Caitlyn's duffel bag in the hallway, looking out of breath as he ran his hands through his messy brown hair. "Yours was my favorite audition. So far. There's still a lot more to see, but I bet yours will be the best."

"Thanks." Caitlyn smiled, raising an eyebrow. "You were watching me?"

"I mean, we were watching everyone," Tyler said. "Max and I. He's working the lights and sound today. I've been helping out…which is probably more information than you needed." He moved aside as Caitlyn hoisted her bag.

Her stomach grumbled. "I don't suppose the diner across the street takes IOUs?"

"You know what, lemme help you out." Tyler pulled a smartphone out of a pocket in his cargo pants. "Just gonna let Max know where I'm going."

"Oh no, I didn't mean—it's fine. I'm sure I've got enough for a bagel or something." Her cheeks reddened as her stomach growled again. "I don't need anyone to rescue me."

Tyler frowned at something on his phone. "I'm no hero," he said, looking back up at Caitlyn. "It's just breakfast."

"Okay, but next time is on me."

Next time, Tyler mused as he watched Caitlyn devour her eggs Benedict. They sat across from each other in a booth with fraying red leather seats at the small diner next to the theater. He pushed aside the admonishments Max had texted him about patterns and toxic people, choosing to leave his phone on silent during their meal.

Caitlyn was toxic like… like dandelions were toxic.

Wait, dandelions aren't toxic, are they?

Tyler had a vague recollection of his parents yelling at him not to blow on them when he was a little kid because the seeds went everywhere. But he was also pretty sure dandelions were edible.

Edible…what?!

"Are you okay?" Caitlyn looked concerned, holding a precarious forkful of hashbrowns.

Tyler felt his cheeks redden. "Yeah, I'm fine," he said. "I'm more worried about you. I mean, I'm not *worried* about you. I just mean… well, what are you gonna do? About your living situation?"

"I dunno," she said through a bite. "I guess I'll go to one of those women's shelters or something and start looking up ads for roommates. Probably find someplace new in a day or two." Her words sounded confident enough, and she smiled, but it didn't reach her downcast eyes.

"We have a couch," Tyler blurted out.

Caitlyn furrowed her brow.

"Max and I have an apartment a few blocks away. Just one bedroom, but there's a couch in the living room. May even be room for your duffle bag." Tyler smiled. Then he reached into his pocket and pulled out a key. "I gotta go back, but I'll give you the address."

Caitlyn considered, then reached for the key. "Thank you. I promise to get out of your hair as soon as I can."

"Take all the time you need."

Max is gonna kill me.

. . .

Caitlyn entered the apartment and took a step past the no-butt kitchen into what passed for the living room. Grateful to get her heavy bag off her shoulders, she peered around, getting the lay of the land. She caught a glimpse of a bunk bed through the bedroom door. The entire apartment could fit into the living room and kitchen of Dominique's apartment. Still, to be this close to the hustle and bustle of Times Square?

Worth it.

It was clean, too. Her dad always kept the house clean even after her mother was gone, but Caitlyn thought bachelors were supposed to be messy. She was an absolute slob compared to these two. She made a mental note to stay on top of things as long as Tyler and Max let her crash at their place.

Caitlyn did *not* want to overstay her welcome.

She collapsed onto the faded leather couch, wishing she had her blanket. Her phone beeped. Caitlyn slipped it out of her hoodie. A text from Dominique asking where she was, and if she was okay. She smirked as she tapped out a reply. *I'm basically staying in Times Square at the moment. If you bring my bedding to work, I can stop by tomorrow to pick it up,* she texted back.

K, Dominique replied minutes later.

Caitlyn rolled over and fell asleep.

"I thought I told you not to bring home any strays."

Tyler rolled his eyes at Max's back as he walked behind him into the apartment. "You hungry?" he said to Caitlyn, who sat up on the couch, stretching. Tyler reached for a folding table against the wall and set it up. Max set down a few sodas and a box of pizza on the table before sinking into a mismatched suede armchair. Caitlyn made room on the couch for Tyler. "We didn't know what you liked, so we just got cheese."

"No problem." Caitlyn smiled. "How did the rest of the auditions go?"

"Honestly," Tyler said, "your group was probably one of the best overall, but there were some standouts here and there. You probably have a good shot, though," he was quick to add. "Maya, maybe Anne Marie…"

"I know she has the more impressive resume, and I swear I'm not just saying this out of jealousy or whatever, but I really didn't like her audition," Caitlyn blurted out.

"Right?" Max said, acknowledging Caitlyn directly for the first time. "Acoustic reinterpretations of pop songs are so overdone. Bet she just copied someone she saw online, too. But she's probably moving on to the next round of auditions, whether we like it or not."

"Max used to perform in high school, so he can be a bit critical," Tyler added.

Max gave him a warning look, but Caitlyn didn't notice. "Really? What roles did you play?"

Max appeared defiant as his eyes returned to Caitlyn's face. "My best part was probably Roxie Hart."

Caitlyn's eyes widened. "I've always wanted to do *Chicago*."

Max relaxed.

The next morning, Dominique sent another text: *Why don't we meet for lunch? My treat.* After a disappointing morning of searching ads for roommates, Caitlyn didn't feel eager to see her again. Not without good news to share. If only she didn't have to wait until tomorrow to hear back about the show, assuming she survived the first round of cuts.

Tyler and Max were back at Blackstone Theater for the men's auditions. *A singing Van Helsing.* Caitlyn tried to imagine it while she showered. Jonathon would probably have some drippy ballad with Mina. A show-stopping number between Lucy and her suitors. Maybe even a tango. *That* she could see. As she washed her hair, envisioned being spun between three faceless men, then chided herself for getting too far ahead of herself. One of the faceless men flung her into the arms of…*Tyler?*

What?

No, no, no, no, no, no.

Caitlyn's eyes opened wide. As if the universe itself wanted to punish her, some soap got in her eyes. She whimpered as she rinsed them out. Then Caitlyn turned off the water and grabbed a towel.

"It didn't look like it was going to rain when I got here," Dominique said when Caitlyn sat across from her at their favorite sushi restaurant. The dark wood table tops and leather seats looked expensive, but the food was cheap, by New York City standards anyway. "I hope it's okay, I ordered for you. Your usual."

Despite the dim lighting, Caitlyn felt self-conscious. Her hair was still damp and hung in limp waves around her face. "I gotta get a hair dryer. Turns out men aren't big with hair appliances." Caitlyn tucked a strand of hair behind her ear and forced a smile. She took the lid off her miso soup and reached for a spoon.

"You have male roommates?" Dominique looked surprised.

"Still looking for the right place," Caitlyn said, "but a couple techies from the theater are letting me crash at their place in the meantime."

"Are you sure that's a good idea?" Now Dominique sounded concerned.

One corner of Caitlyn's lips dropped in mild annoyance. "They're nice," she said. "They've been nothing but perfect gentlemen." Dominique didn't need to know about any intrusive thoughts she'd been having.

That could become a problem, but Caitlyn pushed her silly fantasies aside.

Dominique remained doubtful, but she let the issue rest while they ate. Instead, she talked about work and Harper's boyfriend. Naomi had talked Dominique into placing a bet on how long it would last. "Harper's certain he's the one," she said, shrugging. "I'm happy for her. I really am. I just hope he's not another player like the last one. These rich boys. They're used to getting what they want when they want it."

"That's why I only date bums like me!"

"Catie…"

Caitlyn's phone beeped before she could reassure Dominique that she was kidding. "Omigod," she said, staring at the text. "Omigod, omigod, omigod."

"What is it? What's wrong?"

Caitlyn all but danced in her chair when she clasped the phone to her chest and looked up at Dominique, grinning like a loon. "Tyler—he's one of the techies—he caught a glimpse of the director's notepad with my name highlighted. And so were some of the best women who auditioned yesterday, so he's pretty sure I'm getting called back."

"That's great," Dominique said. "I hope you'll let me know when it's official."

Caitlyn was still riding high from Tyler's message when she returned to his apartment, but doubt crept in as she sat down on the couch and hugged her bedding to her chest. A lot could happen between now and tomorrow.

What if Elliot changed his mind?

four

. . .

"I've never seen someone eat so many donut holes in one sitting." Tyler looked either horrified or impressed. Caitlyn couldn't tell.

"I told you not to tell her anything," Max said, taking a sip of his coffee. He reached for a couple more donut holes—before Caitlyn could eat them all, no doubt—and sat down on the couch beside Tyler.

Tyler frowned. "I thought it would help take the edge off."

Max gestured at Caitlyn's powder-dusted lips as evidence to the contrary.

"Guys, I'm fine." Caitlyn wiped her face with a napkin. Her phone betrayed her when it beeped and she almost fell out of the chair trying to get to it. "It's just a message from my dad," she said, looking up at them, stone-faced. Max shook his head and Tyler sat on the couch with a sigh.

A smile spread across Caitlyn's face. "Kidding. Callbacks are tonight at seven."

Caitlyn seemed happier to Tyler but appeared no less nervous as the day wore on. She insisted on walking to Central Park in the afternoon to stretch and practice since there was no room in the apartment. "Are you sure it's safe?" he asked.

"It's the middle of the day." Caitlyn stood, defiant, with her hands on her hips. "I'm no stranger to going it alone."

"I know," Tyler said. "I've just been hearing stories about animals acting weird. The raccoons are getting really aggressive." He ignored the incredulous look Max gave him on his way into the bedroom. Max sat on the bottom bunk and opened his laptop. Tyler remembered he needed to do some data entry for his own side hustle.

"I'll try not to get rabies before tonight." Caitlyn tied her hoodie around her waist and walked out the door.

"It's not just the animals acting weird," Max called from the bedroom after she was gone.

"Shut up."

One of the many nice things about Central Park was that Caitlyn had no problem finding plenty of room on the grass to practice dancing without too many strange looks from passersby. She felt grateful for a nice breeze on this unseasonably warm spring day as she slipped off her hoodie and tied it around her waist. She'd pulled her hair back into a tidy braid, having scrounged up a couple hair ties from the bottom of her duffel bag. As tidy as she could manage, anyway.

Caitlyn leapt and twirled without incident until a piercing scream interrupted the rustle of leaves in the trees and distant road noise. A jogger removed his earbuds, looking in the scream's direction but continued running the opposite way. Caitlyn ran toward it instead. Going the other way never even occurred to her as she pushed through some shrubs and entered another clearing. A woman stared in horror at the mangled remains of a...

...is that—was that—a raccoon?

Caitlyn couldn't be sure what it was as she stared at the bloody misshapen mass in front of the woman. *Strange place for roadkill,* she thought to herself, but of course nobody would drag that into the middle of the park... would they?

"What do you suppose happened to it?" The woman's voice shook. "Does this sort of thing happen here a lot?"

A tourist, probably. She had graying hair pulled back into a ponytail, an "I love NY" tee shirt and khakis, a colorful fanny pack at her waist, and an amateur camera slung around her neck.

"Not really," Caitlyn said. The woman still looked pale and out of sorts. "You should probably sit down. If you continue down the path, there's some benches." The woman nodded and wandered away.

In addition to her scrunchie, Caitlyn had also dug up enough loose change from the bottom of her duffel bag to buy a hot dog from a street vendor. Mustard only. Onions seemed too risky in her new cozy—if temporary—dwelling.

She headed back to the apartment, deciding not to mention the dead animal to Tyler. He seemed a little on edge as it was.

"Must be nice to live in walking distance from so many venues," Caitlyn said as she walked with Max and Tyler to the Blackstone Theater later that day. "Not that I plan on cramping your style for too much longer. Three's a crowd and all that."

Honestly, even two people seemed like a crowd in their apartment, but Caitlyn kept that sentiment to herself.

"It's fine," Max said. "Take as long as you need."

Caitlyn groaned inwardly when the first women she saw were Anne Marie and her awful friends, Sophia and Elise. Laurel was a more pleasant surprise, but Maya wasn't a surprise at all. Her whole group had made it through to the next round. Joining them were two dozen more women, some of whom Caitlyn remembered from other off-Broadway shows.

Caitlyn had played a bohemian when Amelia Lopez was a lead in *Rent*. Next to Maya, she probably had the most impressive resume—anda huge vocal range, from what Caitlyn remembered. "I was going to tour with a production of *Hamilton*," Caitlyn overheard her saying, "but my grandmother isn't doing well, so I wanted to stay close to home." The women surrounding her nodded sympathetically.

Anne Marie muttered something about diversity casting to her friends. From the look of disdain Maya shot the woman, Caitlyn suspected she heard it, too. She decided to join Laurel, who kept to herself on the side of the stage.

"Nervous?"

Laurel turned to look at Caitlyn and paused for a moment before answering. "This part makes me more nervous than the actual audition," she said, shrugging in the direction of the stage. "I don't really know what to do with myself when there's no music."

Caitlyn nodded. "Probably best to focus on what's ahead of us instead of getting caught up in all the drama. Anne Marie's making friends already," she added with a wry grin.

Laurel tilted her head. "She isn't very nice."

"No, she isn't," Caitlyn agreed quickly, making a mental note to avoid sarcasm around Laurel.

Two short claps rang out, signaling the start of the audition. "Alright, ladies, let's begin," a voice called out.

Caitlyn gave Laurel a smile of encouragement as they joined the other auditioners on stage. The speaker was an older woman with a graying brown bob and glasses. She smiled and introduced herself as the vocal coach, Diane Law. "But I'm not here to judge you," she assured them, deadpanning. "Just your performance."

The other women groaned or laughed politely.

Diane launched into her instructions. "I'm going to teach you part of Lucy's big solo when she is telling Mina all about her suitors. Remember, this isn't just about hitting the notes but conveying character. And since this is a brand-new production in process, you aren't following in anyone's footsteps. This is your opportunity to make this part your own, and maybe someday yours will be the definitive performance others emulate."

Diane passed out pieces of paper with the music and lyrics. Then she sat down at the piano on a corner of the stage.

Caitlyn studied the sheet music as the auditions began. Lucy was written for a mezzo-soprano with a pop belt. The notes fit comfortably within Caitlyn's range, but also Maya and Amelia's. Anne Marie was a mezzo-soprano without a strong belt, but what she lacked in technical skill, she made up for in showmanship. Her Lucy was bold and bombastic. She even spoke one of the lyrics, perhaps because she feared she couldn't hit the note, but it worked. Yet Maya and Amelia brought a vulnerability to the role that was absent from Anne Marie's performance.

When it was Caitlyn's turn, she tried to temper the brazen sexiness of Anne Marie with the vulnerability of Maya and Amelia. She hit all the notes. Diane looked pleased when she was finished, but Caitlyn worried her performance was uneven and erratic, not unlike Caitlyn herself. She knew Elliot was watching them from the audience somewhere. That's who she really needed to sell the performance to. If only his Mina had been on stage as a foil.

Laurel sounded sweet but lacked the fire Lucy required. Nobody else stood out.

After everyone sang, Isabella came up to the stage to teach them part of the choreography when Lucy is under Dracula's thrall. "To set the scene, Dracula will be singing to Lucy sight unseen. She will rise from her bed to dance the solo I am about to teach you. Eventually she will be joined by the vampire brides, then Dracula himself."

Though it was another contemporary dance like Monday's audition, the solo remained slow and steady throughout, incorporating elements of ballet. Laurel shined. Anne Marie was competent. Maya and Amelia remained the two to beat.

"Who do you think? Maya or Amelia?"

Tyler stared blankly at Caitlyn as they left the theater.

"Maya," Max said. "Amelia's great, but my money's on Maya."

"Oh. To play Lucy." Tyler smacked his head. "I think Caitlyn has a shot."

"Oh, no, you were wonderful," Max said, side-stepping a couple tourists posing for a selfie in the middle of the sidewalk. "But this is a brand-new production, and they already cast an unknown actress as Mina. They'll want more star power for Lucy."

Tyler stopped muttering about tourists, but still looked annoyed as he glanced at Max.

"That's what I'm thinking," Caitlyn said, unoffended. "I'll be thrilled if I get to be one of the vampire brides, but it would be enough to make the chorus."

"Would it, though?" Max asked, stopping in front of the apartment building.

Caitlyn considered her financial situation, a sinking feeling in the pit of her stomach.

She didn't answer.

five

· ꜜ ·

The next day, Caitlyn did not have to wait long for confirmation that Elliot wanted her to come back on Friday. "It's going to be a long day," she told Max and Tyler over sandwiches at the apartment. "First there's paperwork to fill out, a contract—hopefully I get paid sooner rather than later so I can chip in for rent—then they'll start auditioning us against the guys, and in trios to see how well we harmonize with each other. I'm really excited to see the guys."

Tyler's lips twitched.

Max raised an eyebrow at him before turning to Caitlyn. "We saw some pretty good auditions on Tuesday. Looking forward to seeing who makes the final cut. I still think the idea is lame as hell, but the talent might make up for it."

"I think it's going to be amazing," Caitlyn said. "I really like what I've heard of the music, and Isabella Moreno is one of the best choreographers in the business. I wanted to attend her dance studio, but it hasn't really been in the budget."

"If the pay's good enough, maybe you can start setting aside some money to save up for a laptop. You could find some part-time work online like Max and me?"

"Maybe," she mused. But she couldn't squash down her budding hope.

"So, what do you think?"

"I think it's going to be a long night," Max said, turning up the volume on the microphone. He leaned back in his chair and crossed his arms across his chest and his feet at the ankles as he watched the men take turns singing.

"No, I mean about Caitlyn." Tyler ran his hand through his hair.

"I like her, but she can't be comfortable staying on the couch forever. Plus, I think I might have a bit of a crush on her, and it could get awkward if she ever joins me on the bottom bunk," Max added with a sly smile.

"I'm sorry, what?!" Tyler swiveled his chair to glare at Max.

Max laughed.

Tyler deflated. "Is it that obvious?"

"Only to me," Max said. "She's oblivious."

"What am I gonna do?"

"As long as she's staying with us, there's nothing you can do," Max said. "It wouldn't be fair to anyone, least of all Caitlyn. So, get it together. You're making it weird."

Tyler nodded. He turned to watch the auditions, feeling suddenly glum.

The following afternoon, Caitlyn stared down at the contract as she sat in a faded armchair in what passed for the business office of the Blackstone Theater. The nameplate on the large oak desk read Manny Ortega, but right now a woman stood behind it. The dated wooden office furniture appeared clean and recently polished, and the smell of artificial lemon combatted the mustier smell of old carpet.

"As you can see, there's bonus pay depending on the size of your role," Carol's personal assistant, Kristy, explained as she leaned over the table to point to different parts of the contract with a pen. "It can fluctuate throughout the workshopping process if your part gets bigger or smaller. That's why we ask that everyone commit at the base rate of pay, but it's competitive because we know we're demanding a lot of your time."

"Looks good," Caitlyn said, lifting her own pen.

Kristy sat back. "This was one of my easier signings," she said, looking relieved.

Caitlyn bit her lip. She hoped that wasn't a bad sign. The pay looked reasonable enough. And it was more than she'd made per week on any production so far. She could contribute rent money and still have enough left over for food.

"Tyler!" Caitlyn called out as she passed him in the hall. "I'm in! I got a contract!"

"That's good," Tyler said, looking distracted. "You're still searching for another place, though, right?"

Caitlyn nodded, hurt. She thought Tyler liked her, and even Max seemed to be warming up to her, but maybe she had already overstayed her welcome. Caitlyn didn't have time to dwell on it because callbacks were beginning soon. She walked backstage to join a growing crowd of men and women. Maya and Amelia, of course, and Anne Marie and her friends, but also Laurel and three other women. Emma Taylor was an incredible dancer like Laurel. Stronger singer, too, but an alto. The other two, Cassidy Chase and Jennifer Williams, also had lower voices, so they might round out the trio of vampire brides—but Lucy's part was out of their range.

Unless Elliot or James Merrick, the man with whom he was writing the music and lyrics, decided to change it. The show was a work in progress, after all; and, like Kristy had indicated during their meeting, anything and everything was subject to change.

"Hey, I know you," someone said behind Caitlyn. She turned to face Nicholas Pagonis. Like Anne, he had been a lead in *A Chorus Line*, but Caitlyn had never talked to him for any length of time before. He had been too busy working his way through the rest of the women in the cast from what she remembered. "Cathy, right?" His green eyes sparkled as he gazed at her face.

"Caitlyn," she corrected with a wry grin. "Didn't you play Mike Costa in *A Chorus Line*?" The cocky, flirtatious performer role hadn't been much of a stretch for Nicholas.

Nicholas grinned. "You remembered." He ran his hand through his dark wavy hair in what Caitlyn imagined was meant as a show of humility. Then he caught sight of someone over her shoulder. "Break a leg," he said, briefly meeting her eyes and touching her arm before moving on to an unimpressed Maya.

"Such an ass," Caitlyn heard Anne Marie mumble.

No love lost between those two, she suspected. Caitlyn shrugged and turned to watch as Elliot climbed the steps to join them on stage. Everyone went quiet.

"Okay, ladies," he said. "As the gentlemen already know, the roles of Dracula, Van Helsing, and Renfield were cast early on during the development of our show. I'm not sure our producers would have signed on had I not secured the great Andre Petrov for the titular role." Carol Johansson chuckled in the audience as the women turned to look at each other with excited smiles. "Johan de Jaagar is well known across Europe and making his US debut as Van Helsing, and Renfield will be played by famed character actor Lloyd Berger. You'll meet them next week, I'm sure. Tonight, we will begin by focusing on Lucy and her suitors."

Elliot asked four performers, including Maya and Nicholas, to stay on stage to begin. Caitlyn joined Laurel a few rows back in the auditorium. Nicholas read for the Texan heartthrob Quincy Morris first. Caitlyn could barely contain her giggles as Nicholas attempted an exaggerated southern drawl. Elliot kept Nicholas on stage but switched his part to Lucy's fiancé, Arthur Holmwood. Nicholas looked visibly relieved.

By the time Caitlyn was called up to read for Lucy, clear favorites had emerged as the suitors: Nicholas as Arthur, a lanky sandy-haired man in glasses named Matthew Bauer as the doctor John Seward, and a lean but muscular Christopher Nguyen as Quincy.

"Great job on the accent," Caitlyn told Christopher offstage. "It really sounded authentic."

"I just moved here from Houston," he said, grinning. "I'm afraid I've been type-casted."

She laughed.

Caitlyn grew more anxious as Elliot moved on from acting to singing. He tried all sorts of different groupings. Right now, she was on stage with Emma and Amelia, singing the high part. They sounded good together, even if Caitlyn felt a bit strained.

Before she attempted a high C, a light came crashing to the stage.

Glass shattered everywhere.

Emma and Amelia screamed.

Caitlyn stared at the broken light at her feet, trembling in shock.

"Max! Tyler!" Elliot bellowed. "Get up on the catwalk and see what happened!"

"If that had landed on her head…"

Tyler frowned as he walked along the catwalk with Max, holding a flashlight.

"Don't even think about it," Max said. "Let's just make sure the rest of the lights are secure." He continued forward, then stopped where the light had fallen. "Shit!" he hissed under his breath. "What the hell?"

"Something bit it clean through," Tyler said, looking at the frayed cable. "A rat couldn't have done that, could it?"

"I dunno," Max said. "Let's check the rest."

"Are you okay?" Nicholas walked to Caitlyn, wrapping an arm around her and turning her toward him with his free hand.

"My dad always said I had a voice that could bring down the house," she said.

Nicholas laughed. "Let's get you some water."

• • •

"How much is that going to cost?"

Carol Johansson's brows knitted together. Max and Tyler had just finished describing the damage to the cords securing the lights.

"Much less than a wrongful death suit," Elliot told her. "But Manny should take care of the expense. It's his building. Right?" He turned to Max and Tyler for confirmation, but they shrugged.

"You'll have to call him," Tyler said.

Elliot ran a hand through his hair and blew out a breath. Then he rose. "Alright, ladies and gentlemen, I'm afraid we'll be ending tonight's audition sooner than we planned. But I think we've seen all that we need to reach some preliminary decisions. A tentative cast list will be posted when you arrive Monday morning."

"Are you okay?" Elliot asked, approaching Caitlyn backstage as the performers gathered their things to leave.

She forced a smile. "I'm fine," she said. "I was just a little startled."

"Good," he said warmly, squeezing her shoulder. "We can't have a show without you."

Caitlyn's jaw dropped as she watched him go.

That was a good sign, right?

six

. . .

"**D**id I do something wrong?"

Tyler looked up from his cereal in surprise. Caitlyn sat across from him on the couch, her hair still wet from her shower. "You mean last night? With the light? It was an accident. Besides, you were on stage."

"Not that." Caitlyn shook her head. "Just seems like you're in a hurry to get rid of me."

"What? Oh, no." Tyler gave her what he hoped passed for a reassuring smile. "I just feel bad you have to sleep on the couch. Feels wrong to collect rent when you don't even have your own room. That's all."

"Okay." Caitlyn looked unconvinced. "Anyway, I do have some places I'm checking out this weekend. So, I won't be around much. Just wanted to, you know, touch base. Make sure everything is still okay."

"Everything's fine," Tyler told her. "Really." He considered touching her hand, but decided against it, giving her another crooked smile instead. She didn't return it. Tyler sighed inwardly.

. . .

In truth, Caitlyn wasn't having much luck in the roommate department. Most places were out of her budget, or the other renters wanted payment up front as a show of good faith. Still, she couldn't sit around the apartment all weekend. And she was worried Tyler had picked up on some sort of vibe from her, and that's why he was acting strange.

A headline caught her eye as she passed a newsstand on the way to Central Park. "Influencer abducted by aliens and replaced by an imposter!" it proclaimed. Caitlyn rolled her eyes. Clearly the preferred publication of her buddy on the subway last week.

An older woman in a gray cardigan and darker gray pants paused beside Caitlyn, adjusting her glasses. "The way things are going, I wouldn't be surprised to find out aliens really have been living among us all along, learning to blend in and infiltrate our neighborhoods. Kind of like Russian spies in the eighties, though I suppose that was before your time. Crazy, right?"

The woman's words gave her a chill. "I've heard crazier," Caitlyn said, offering a shaky smile.

Caitlyn pushed aside her unease as she walked, trying to enjoy the sights and sounds of the city. She walked by a well-dressed child while a professional photographer took pictures and asked questions of the child like he was a minor celebrity. The mother stood by with a look of pride. Businesspeople, students, and tourists alike hurried across busy intersections. Drivers laid on their horns or hollered out their windows, some for no other reason than because they could, and because it was expected of them.

Whatever the cast list revealed on Monday, Caitlyn was happy to stay in this crazy unpredictable city. She didn't fit in here anymore than she fit in at home, but nobody fit in here, and that's why everybody belonged. Even the strange man wearing a black suit and a blond buzzcut, who turned to watch as she walked past. Especially him.

She kept going without giving him a second thought.

"That's the third one this week," a city employee complained as he shoveled something unrecognizable into a garbage can outside the park.

"I did hear something on the news about animal attacks getting worse with global warming," said another.

"Global warming's a crock," retorted the first.

The sound of their bickering faded as Caitlyn ventured deeper into the park. She walked without a clear destination in mind until she found herself in front of the Alice in Wonderland statue. Caitlyn watched small children climb atop the mushrooms to sit beside Alice and Dinah and gaze in wonder at the other characters. She thought the Cheshire cat winked at her. Caitlyn took a deep breath and wiped the sweat from her brow.

"You know, coming to New York City isn't all that different from stepping through the looking glass," someone said in a smooth drawl behind her. Caitlyn turned to face Christopher. He appeared unfazed by yet another unseasonably warm spring day, standing there in his faded jeans and a blue tee shirt that accentuated his slim, muscular build without looking like he was trying too hard.

"And you should always be careful before accepting food or drink from strangers," Caitlyn attempted to quip. *Or maybe that was just for women—and pretty much went for anywhere.* She pursed her lips, considering. Christopher chuckled anyway. Caitlyn relaxed and gave him a curious smile. "Doing the tourist thing?"

Christopher nodded. "Don't suppose you could help me find the zoo? The big cats are my favorite. We don't have any snow leopards in Houston."

Caitlyn had a sneaking suspicion Christopher didn't need her help, but she also didn't mind accompanying him. "You're stuck with me for a while. It's at the other end of the park. Limited admission, though. Do you have a ticket?"

"As luck would have it, I have two. Hotel deal." Christopher grinned. "I didn't want to commit to an apartment until I knew something for sure. I've heard the city will eat you alive if you don't have a plan. Literally, some might say. A couple of the other guys were looking for a new roommate, though, so I'm moving in with them on Monday after the read-through."

"I'm between apartments myself," Caitlyn said as they walked.

"You're not from around here, either, are you?" Christopher gazed at her.

"Ohio," Caitlyn said. "I moved here a year ago. Things haven't been going well lately—but I'm used to pushing through tough times," she was quick to add. "My dad can't decide if I'm persistent or just stubborn, but I tell him I have to keep swimming, or I'll die."

"Like a shark," Christopher said, his face solemn, though the corners of his eyes crinkled with amusement.

"Like a shark," Caitlyn agreed.

———

Caitlyn giggled as a baby goat nibbled feed out of the palm of her hand. In the last two hours, she'd learned that Christopher was the baby of the family. His older brother taught high school and his older sister was a physical therapist, whereas Christopher had been voted Most Likely to Win an Oscar by his classmates. Carol Johannson had happened to see him as Seymour in *Little Shop of Horrors* at his community college when visiting one of her children. She'd invited him to New York to audition for Elliot's musical.

Caitlyn also learned that Laurel was looking to move out of her parents' home on Staten Island. She made a mental note to do a better job asking people about their lives—and to talk to Laurel about maybe renting an apartment together.

"Here's looking at you, Kid," Christopher said as he nudged a baby goat off his lap.

Caitlyn groaned.

"Really? I was proud of myself when I thought it up a few minutes ago." Christopher pretended to pout. He grudgingly accepted Caitlyn's hand when she offered it and rose to his feet. He held on a moment longer to say, "I had a nice time today. We should have dinner one of these days."

Caitlyn felt her cheeks flush. "Definitely," she said.

. . .

When Caitlyn banged through the door, her face was all splotchy and windblown. "Did you run a marathon?" Tyler asked from the suede chair.

She didn't move, just stared at him.

"You look like you went for a run." He gestured at his own face and hair.

Caitlyn's eyes widened, and she ran into the bathroom. When she returned with her hair in a less messy ponytail, she said, "I ran into Chris—Christopher Nguyen—at the park. Then we went to the zoo." She walked to the fridge and lifted out a bottle of water.

"Oh," Tyler said. "Neat."

Max was sitting across from him on the couch. Tyler could feel him staring, but he pointedly avoided making eye contact. "So, it sounds like Manny got someone out right away to take care of the lights. Also called an exterminator, but he didn't notice any signs of an infestation…well, no worse than the usual rat here or there, anyway. It's still the city."

"Sure, there's no signs of an infestation…if you ignore all the cables being chewed all to hell," Max said.

"Do you still think it was just rats?"

Max looked at Caitlyn. "If it wasn't rats, I don't know what else it could have been."

seven

. . .

Caitlyn spent Sunday wandering around the city again, but without any chance encounters. She even checked out a couple of apartments, but the rent was too high for one, and the other…well, Caitlyn had a sneaking suspicion her prospective roommates were squatters seeking someone to supplement their lifestyle. By the time Sunday night rolled around, she was back to thinking about the show.

Max and Tyler struggled to keep up with Caitlyn as they walked to the theater the next morning. By the time they arrived, a small crowd had gathered around the back door. Sophia and Elise were congratulating Anne Marie, who looked annoyed, and Maya and Amelia were talking to each other in low voices. Nicholas stood off to the side, shaking his head with a bemused smile. Caitlyn squeezed beside the other women to look at the list posted on the door.

Anne Marie had been cast as Lucy.

Really?

Caitlyn looked below her to see Maya, Amelia, and Emma as Dracula's brides. Her heart sank. Someone touched her shoulder. She turned to look at Christopher, hoping he wouldn't notice the tears blurring her vision.

"For what it's worth," he said, "you were my favorite to read with."

Caitlyn forced a shaky smile. "Congratulations," she said. "Congratulations, right?" She double checked to confirm that Christopher had in fact been cast as Quincy. Nicholas and Matthew had been cast as the fiancé and doctor, as expected, with someone named Michael Harris playing Jonathon Harker. Caitlyn remembered a slight young man with pretty blond waves extending past his jaw and a beautiful tenor voice. Christopher nodded, placing a hand on her back as they walked into the theater. His gentle touch took the edge off Caitlyn's disappointment over her minor role in the ensemble, if only for the brief moment it lasted.

"I thought for sure it would be you, me, and Emma with Maya as Lucy," Amelia said as they walked into the green room of the theater, where chairs had been arranged in a large circle for the read-through. She slipped on a pair of reading glasses as she sat down.

Caitlyn sat between Amelia and Laurel. Elliot sat across from them. To his right sat a handsome thirty-something man with piercing blue eyes and hair that was just beginning to gray at the temples, though his face remained relatively unlined. To Elliot's left sat a man in his forties with a mop of blond hair and a craggy but friendly face. Beside that man sat a slender pallid man of indeterminate age with unruly brown hair. After he introduced Andre Petrov, Johan de Jaager, and Lloyd Berger, Elliot asked the rest of the cast to introduce themselves and their characters.

"Laurel Locke," the dancer said softly when it was her turn. "Um, I'm just in the chorus."

"Don't be so modest," Elliot interrupted. "The chorus is integral to bringing Victorian London to life. And remember, this show is a work in progress. Nobody is safe. Watch out for these girls," he said to Anne Marie. "They're still auditioning for your role."

The actress smirked like she wasn't all that concerned.

Elliot turned his attention to Caitlyn. "And how are you after Friday's little scare?"

"I'm Caitlyn Smith. Chorus," she said. "Oh, and I'm fine. Really. Thanks." She looked down at the script in her hands, noticing it was already beginning to wrinkle.

"Good, good," Elliot said, before introductions continued.

Caitlyn tried to focus on the read-through, but with so little to do besides listen, she became lost in her thoughts. First, she replayed all her auditions from the previous week, trying to pinpoint where she'd gone wrong—as if it mattered now. Then she considered her volatile living situation and whether she should even think about going out with Chris at a time like this.

"Caitlyn, are you okay?"

Caitlyn looked over at Laurel, startled. Then she looked around the room, realizing it was empty. "Where'd everybody go?"

"Breaking for lunch," Laurel said. "There's pizza in the hall. I brought my own food."

"Oh, right."

She left the green room to grab a slice of pizza, but she didn't have much of an appetite. Her mind was still occupied through lunch and into the afternoon. Diane Law finally started teaching the ensemble a few songs, and it felt good to sing and be amongst other performers. In addition to sweet Laurel, Jennifer and Cassidy were funny and friendly. Even Sophia and Elise became more tolerable when Anne Marie was not around. The men in the ensemble seemed nice, too. Relaxed, easygoing, and focused on work.

Still, Caitlyn was relieved when rehearsal came to an end. She trudged up to the control booth to meet Max and Tyler.

"Clearly Elliot is a sociopath," Max said when she walked in.

"I'm disappointed for Caitlyn, too, but that feels like a stretch," Tyler said.

"Oh, you deserved better," Max said. "But I'm talking about casting bitter exes opposite of eachother. I mean, it's not like Elliot knew what went down during *A Chorus Line*, but you saw how callbacks went.

You could cut the tension between Anne Marie and Nick with a knife. And it's not the sexy 'will they or won't they' kind. Now your problem, if there was one, is that you had the best chemistry with Chris, but I suppose the audience could have assumed Lucy made the responsible choice instead of the passiona—"

"There's really no sense in dwelling on it," Tyler interrupted. "What do you want to eat for dinner? Your choice," he said to Caitlyn.

"I'm not that hungry," she said. "Lunch made my stomach grumpy."

"How long do you think she's going to mope?"

Max shrugged out of his hoodie, glaring. "I don't know. I'm not the actress whisperer."

"But you have experience with the performance side of things," Tyler said. "All the backstage drama and stuff. I'm just the sound guy. My biggest disappointment is the time I got stuck in here with Billy running the lights on Taco Tuesday."

"Forty years old, and he still lives at home." Max changed into pajama bottoms. "I dunno, Ty. Hopefully she snaps out of it sooner rather than later. It's still anyone's game, anyway. I don't think she should chip in for a whole third of the rent while she's crashing on the couch, though. Maybe just a couple hundred. That seems reasonable."

"Sounds fair," Tyler agreed, climbing the ladder to the top bunk. He heard the bottom bunk squeak as his roommate got comfortable. "Hey, Max?"

"Yeah…?"

"Chris isn't all that attractive, is he?"

"He's ripped, he sounds like Matthew McConaughey, and he has cheekbones to die for. But other than that, he may as well be Billy the Blaster."

Tyler didn't answer. Not long after, Max was snoring.

eight

. . .

A few days later, Caitlyn sat with her fellow castmates in the women's dressing room, in between singing with Diane and dancing with Isabella.

"Gah, he's so hot." Emma tugged on a strand of auburn hair and bit her lip.

"Chris?" Caitlyn tried to keep her face neutral as she regarded Emma's reflection in the wall-length mirror.

"Oh, he's cute, too, but I meant Matt."

"She has a thing for men in glasses," Jennifer explained, pulling her dark blond hair back into a ponytail. "Now Leanne is more my type."

Cassidy smacked her arm. Jennifer tucked a loose strand of her girlfriend's raven hair behind her ear with an affectionate look.

"Things seem pretty serious between her and Elliot," Maya said. She leaned over in her chair to tie her shoes. "She definitely didn't score the part on star power alone."

"Oh, she's not that bad," Amelia said. "She can carry a tune."

"And Michael and Anne Marie will have to carry all her scenes," Emma said. "Her most convincing performance will be when she's sleepwalking." Maya laughed, and even Amelia bit her lip on a giggle.

"Where's Sophia and Elise?" Laurel interrupted, looking uncomfortable.

Maya rolled her eyes. "Anne Marie claimed one of the private dressing rooms," she said. "They're probably with her."

Caitlyn bumped into Leanne backstage. Literally.

The actress turned to stare. Her dark eyes appeared almost haunted as she asked, "Have you ever felt all wrong in your own body?" She held up her hands, flexing her slender fingers.

"Is that from the script?" Caitlyn asked.

"What?" Leanne gave her head a little shake, appearing more lucid. "Oh, no. I'm sorry. I'm having sort of a weird day."

"Tell me about it."

They walked on stage as Isabella was directing Emma, Maya, and Amelia back to the green room to continue working with Diane. "Today you'll start learning the choreography for the ballroom scene when Lucy introduces Mina to her suitors," she explained to the rest of them. "I won't sugarcoat things. This is the most complex choreography in the show. It begins as a Viennese waltz but transitions into a quickstep with six revolving pairs of dancers swapping partners."

The women exchanged looks. In addition to Nicholas, Matthew, and Christopher, there were only three other men.

"I see you're doing the math," Isabella said with a smile. "The scene opens with Lucy and Mina descending the stairs. As Lucy and Mina sing, the rest of you will be waltzing. When that song ends and transitions into the next, two ladies will step out and Mina and Lucy will step in. That's when the fun begins."

Caitlyn groaned inwardly. Though she had taken ballroom dance classes, the quickstep in particular was a killer. But heady excitement replaced her trepidation when Isabella partnered her with Christopher for the waltz.

"Howdy, stranger," he said as he held out his hand.

"Howdy!" Caitlyn grinned up at him.

"I apologize in advance if I step on your feet," he said.

Despite the preemptive apology, Caitlyn found Christopher to be an excellent partner. They glided across the stage effortlessly. She hid a smile as she noticed Nicholas trying to use his charm on Jennifer with Anne Marie glaring at them from upstage. Isabella kept everyone with their original partners as she taught the basics of the quickstep first. Caitlyn stumbled once or twice, but she was having too much fun with Christopher to care.

"A valiant effort," Isabella told Sophia and Elise, "but I think you two can sit this one out when we continue to work on this number tomorrow."

Elise frowned, but Sophia looked relieved.

Caitlyn tried to give Laurel a congratulatory thumbs up, but the dancer was too busy casting furtive glances at her waltz partner. Judging by Matthew's faint smile, Caitlyn could tell he noticed, too.

"Looks like Caitlyn's cheering back up," Max said. They were back up in the booth.

"I noticed," Tyler said.

"Tomorrow Elliot wants me to gel some lights so he can start playing with different schemes," Max said. "You're gonna help out, right?"

"Are you afraid of being alone on the catwalk, too?"

Max raised an eyebrow. "Aren't you?"

Tyler considered the chewed cables of the light that nearly fell on Caitlyn last week. Then there were the strange sounds he'd been hearing. Whatever was scurrying in the walls and along the catwalk seemed bigger than the average city rat. "Honestly, this whole building has been creeping me out lately. And Leanne was weird in the hallway yesterday."

"Yeah, I saw her too. So weird," Max agreed. "I don't suppose you happened to check out her teeth?"

"What, do you think *she* chewed up the cables?" Tyler raised his eyebrows.

Max laughed. "It's New York City. Stranger things have happened."

. . .

"You should let me take you out this weekend," Caitlyn heard Nicholas tell Jennifer after rehearsal. She exchanged a look with Laurel as they stepped out of the dressing room into the hall. Anne Marie stepped out of the room across from them, but it was Leanne's dressing room and not her own. Caitlyn noticed shadows under her eyes that hadn't been there before.

Jennifer glanced in their direction. "I don't think my girlfriend would appreciate that." She left Nicholas standing agape to stride down the hall. "Caitlyn, Laurel, you should totally come out with Cassidy and me tomorrow night. I know one of the bouncers at this new club, The Way Station. It's super-exclusive, but he can get us in." She ignored Anne Marie, who walked to her own dressing room with a thin but satisfied smile.

"The Way Station?" Laurel furrowed her brow. "No, thank you."

"Sounds great!" Caitlyn said.

"Awesome!" Jennifer grinned. "Feel free to dress as crazy as you want. The edgier the better."

Caitlyn frowned. "Oh, I don't really have anything…"

"No problem," Jennifer said. "Just come home with us after rehearsal tomorrow. Bring an overnight bag. I'm sure Cassidy or I have something that will fit you, right, Cass?" She wrapped her arm around Cassidy's waist when the other woman left the dressing room.

"Are you sure you wanna go tomorrow?" Laurel asked when they left.

Caitlyn waved away her concern. "Oh, I've been to gay clubs before. It's no big deal."

"No, it's not…I don't mean *that*," Laurel said. "I've just heard stories about that place, that's all."

Caitlyn hadn't heard of The Way Station before now, and she suspected it didn't take much to worry Laurel, living with her parents on Staten Island and all. She remembered she was supposed to talk to Laurel about the possibility of rooming together but couldn't imagine what kind of place they could afford. Instead, she offered her assurances that nothing would happen.

"Nothing bad anyway," she said with a wink.

Someone knocked on the semi-closed door of Max and Tyler's room. Max snapped awake and rubbed the sleep from his eyes. He stumbled to the door and found Caitlyn standing there. "Sorry, I know it's late," she said. "But I forgot I needed to pack an overnight bag, and all I have is my big ol' duffle bag."

There was a creak as Tyler sat up in the top bunk.

"For…?" Max asked.

"Jennifer invited me to go out with her and Cassidy to some new club tomorrow. I'm staying overnight, so I just need to pack a few things."

"Uh huh."

Max rooted through a drawer under the bunk bed and returned with a small satchel before pushing the door shut and climbing back into bed.

"I have to compete with women now, too?" Tyler muttered.

"So, all that stuff I said the other day about getting it together and not making it weird just went in one ear and out the other, is that it?" No answer. "Whatever, it's fine," Max mumbled into his pillow. "Sleep is overrated."

nine

. . .

"So, what do you think about grabbing dinner tonight?" Christopher twirled Caitlyn away, then pulled her back in close. "The guys were telling me about this Latin restaurant in Queens that's sure to rival the food back home, and I can't wait to tell them how wrong they are."

"That sounds great," Caitlyn said as they glided across the stage past Laurel and Matthew. Then she slapped her forehead. "I can't."

"Not the response I was hoping for." Chris gave Caitlyn a rueful grin.

"Totally forgot. I'm going out with Jen and Cass tonight. What about tomorrow?"

His grin widened. "Tomorrow works."

"God damn it, Nick. Stop stepping on my feet!"

Everyone stopped dancing and turned to stare. Anne Marie untangled herself from Nicholas and stormed offstage, tossing her hair over her shoulder with a dramatic flick. "I can't work like this!"

"She'll be in her dressing room," Nicholas quipped when the music came to an abrupt stop, though he looked chagrined rather than his usual cool and impish self.

Isabella sighed. Then she walked to Nicholas. "I guess I'll fill in for now. We really need to work on the transition into the quickstep. A few more minutes, and she would have been switching to a new partner, at least until closer to the end." Isabella looked up at the control booth. "Tyler, start the music back up at the two-and-a-half-minute mark!"

Caitlyn was sorry to separate from Christopher but enjoyed dancing with Matthew and even Nicholas for a few measures. Even the three men from the chorus made fine partners. Isabella put her back with Christopher at the end of the song. Caitlyn was pleased to have a more prominent role than the other women in the chorus.

After rehearsal, Leanne made a beeline for Anne Marie's dressing room. Elise and Sophia huddled together in a corner of the main dressing room instead, talking in low voices to one another. "The leading ladies are becoming pretty close," Amelia said as she entered the room.

Elise looked up. "You mean Anne Marie and Leanne?"

Amelia nodded.

"Anne Marie said she just wants to develop a convincing bond for the show, but she's barely said a word to us all week. And when she does, it's just to complain about Nick or gush about Leanne," Sophia said. "It's boring."

"Gotta say I never got that vibe from Anne Marie," Jennifer said.

"Clearly Leanne inspires people to take all sorts of chances," Maya observed, smirking.

"She does have a great look," Jennifer said. "I just mean, with all that hair and those dark expressive eyes, she looks the part," she assured a frowning Cassidy. "Maybe she's one of those performers who needs an audience to connect."

"That's quite the leap of faith," Amelia said.

Jennifer shrugged and turned to Caitlyn. "You ready?"

She nodded, shouldering the satchel Max had lent her.

"Be careful," Laurel said in a low voice as she walked by.

Caitlyn turned to give her a reassuring grin. "I'll be fine. See you Monday."

. . .

"Here, try these on." Jennifer stepped back from the closet with a pile of clothes. She dropped them on the bed.

Caitlyn looked up from her phone, which had a low battery. She considered asking to use Jennifer's charger, but she was distracted when she spotted a small leather mini skirt on top of the pile of clothes. "I hate skirts," she said, setting aside her phone. "Too drafty."

Jennifer laughed.

After trying on a few things, Caitlyn settled on a pair of slim black pants and a strapless dark red corset. The satiny fabric was snug, but it had a good stretch to it, with boning down the sides for aesthetics only.

"Dunno about your shoes with that outfit, but I don't think we have anything in your size," Jennifer said.

"Comfort is way more important when you're out dancing all night," Cassidy said. "Besides, I doubt anyone's going to be staring at her feet. You look great," she told Caitlyn. "You should let me do your hair and makeup."

By the time Cassidy was done using Caitlyn like a living Barbie doll, as Jennifer put it, her light brown hair fell over her shoulders in soft curls. Cassidy even insisted on giving her a smokey cat eye and dark red lips, darker even than her crimson corset. "I told you," Cassidy said as they looked at her reflection in the bathroom mirror. "You look gorgeous—not like a little kid who's had one too many cherry popsicles."

"That color suits you," Jennifer agreed. "Now let's go." She had changed out of her dance clothes into fashionably torn jeans and a white crop top that revealed a pierced belly button framed by a tattoo of vines and flowers. Cassidy wore a black mini-dress and thigh-high boots. Caitlyn followed them out of the ground-floor apartment they shared with a third roommate, who was working the night shift at a nearby diner.

Jennifer hailed a taxi. "Where are you ladies headed tonight?" the driver asked, adjusting his baseball cap as he gazed at them in the rearview mirror. He was young, with just a hint of a five o'clock shadow.

"The Way Station," Jennifer said. "You know it?"

The driver let out a low whistle. "I've been hearing some wild stories about that place."

"Why do you think we're going?" Jennifer gave him a wolfish grin.

Caitlyn shifted her weight from one foot to the other as she waited outside the club with Jennifer and Cassidy. The posts securing the velvet rope vibrated from pulsing electronic music inside the club. The bouncers were efficient and relentless as they allowed some people past and rejected others.

"ID?" Caitlyn handed her license to a tall, muscular man. "Wrist," he said dispassionately, handing it back. Caitlyn held out her arm as he affixed a neon green wristband indicating she was under the legal drinking age.

"I like it," Jennifer said.

"It really pulls the outfit together," Cassidy teased.

Inside was a laser light show as a DJ spun music in the center of the main room. Professional dancers in scant sparkling clothing moved on platforms throughout the room, some fast and frenetic, others sultry and seductive. Jennifer's white shirt had a faint purple glow under the blacklights. "I should have worn white!" Cassidy pouted.

"I like you better in black!" Jennifer wrapped an arm around Cassidy's waist and kissed her.

Caitlyn followed them to the dance floor. Once they were swallowed by the sea of bodies swaying and dancing, she found it hard to feel like a third wheel. Instead, Caitlyn lost herself in the music. It felt nice being able to move freely without having to worry about any specific choreography or steps. "This place is awesome!" she shouted at Jennifer, who nodded and grinned and probably had no idea what she'd just said.

Caitlyn started paying more attention to the people surrounding them. It was an eclectic group. Every scene from pop to punk appeared to be represented, even bubble goth. Hair of every color, mohawks that defied gravity. The one thing everyone had in common was that they were all beautiful or striking or just plain weird and otherworldly, even by New York City standards. But even the most outlandish of them seemed to respect everyone else's space. Laurel had been worried for no reason.

Now, Caitlyn had learned years ago that appearances could be deceiving. A high school classmate of hers had been raped by a clean-cut preppy in designer clothing (not that he ever saw any consequences). Meanwhile, some of the strangest and scariest-looking New Yorkers could be perfectly pleasant to be around. Like, the bald guy across the room wearing what appeared to be a spiked dog collar around his throat was probably an absolute puppy dog once you got to know him.

Wait. Did his skin just turn blue?

For a moment, Caitlyn thought she could see the veins inside his bulging biceps. She resisted the urge to rub at her eyes and ruin Cassidy's artistry as the strange man seemed to shimmer and shake like a mirage in the road on a hot summer day. She blinked a few times until she saw a normal— if overly fond of leather—man in a spiky dog collar.

Jennifer touched her shoulder and nodded in the direction of a bar across the room. Caitlyn followed Jennifer and Cassidy off the dance floor. As if by magic, three people rose from three bar stools at the end. Caitlyn chose the last seat, and Jennifer sat beside her.

The bartender, a handsome man with chiseled features, platinum blond hair, and unusual blue eyes that appeared almost violet in the dimly lit club, grinned when he saw the green wristband around Caitlyn's arm. Something about him made her think of the man in the spiky dog collar. She supposed it was the leather pants. "I know the perfect drink for you," the bartender said before Caitlyn could order. She turned to her friends with a look of doubt.

"I've heard they have really good mocktails!" Jennifer reassured her. "I'm starting a tab for the three of us! Get whatever you want." A different model-level-of-gorgeous bartender—a woman with long black cornrows—set something sinister and green in a martini glass with a hollow stem in front of Jennifer.

"That doesn't look like an appletini!" Caitlyn watched as the drink fizzed and smoked.

"It's a green dragon! Cass got the red one!"

Sure enough, the bartender returned with another martini glass, this one filled with a blood- red liquid that similarly fizzed and smoked. "There's dry ice inside the stem," Cassidy explained to Caitlyn. "Cool, huh?"

Caitlyn nodded, still feeling doubtful as she watched the women sip their exotic drinks. She breathed a sigh of relief when her own bartender returned with something pink and benign in a margarita glass rimmed with darker pink sugar. There was even one of those edible orchids. "Hibiscus lemonade," the bartender said, showing impossibly white teeth.

Caitlyn took a tentative sip. "It's good," she said, looking up at him, pleasantly surprised.

He winked and walked down the length of the bar to serve someone else.

Caitlyn swiveled in her leather bar seat to look at the rest of the club. To her right she noted a winding staircase leading up to the VIP area. Caitlyn narrowed her eyes as she watched a blonde in a bright red cocktail dress follow a couple, a man in a dress shirt and pants with dark blond curls and a woman in a silky cream dress with a luxurious black mane, up the stairs.

She leaned toward Jennifer. "Is that Anne Marie?"

Jennifer followed her gaze to the balcony and shrugged. "Don't see her." She turned to whisper something in her girlfriend's ear. Cassidy giggled and gave her a playful swat on the arm. Jennifer rose and held out a hand, and Cassidy followed her back out to the dance floor.

"It's cool," Caitlyn muttered. "I'll just sit here and finish my drink. Alone." She forced a brief smile and shook her head when a couple asked if the seats next to her were taken. Caitlyn turned back to watch the throng of bodies on the dance floor. Some people wore those little eye masks like it was Mardi Gras or a masquerade ball or something. Others wore cat ears or had horns protruding from either side of their foreheads.

It was Halloween every night at The Way Station, apparently.

Caitlyn stared at one woman's horns in particular. They looked less like a cheesy sparkling accessory and more like they were actually growing out either side of her head.

Caitlyn tried not to judge, but she had to admit that some of the more extreme cosmetic surgery makeovers gave her pause. The more Caitlyn observed the crowd, the more she felt like she had fallen into the uncanny valley. People with eyes that glowed like cats or some with more reptilian pupils. Even goat eyes. Why would anyone want goat eyes?

Creepy enough on a goat.

Caitlyn's vision wavered, and she nearly toppled over in her chair. She looked up as the woman sitting next to her touched her arm and asked if she was okay. The woman had that eerie blue glow, like the spiky dog collar man from before, only Caitlyn realized it was merely the blue of veins showing through the woman's strange translucent skin. Then she blinked, and the woman looked normal again.

Somehow Caitlyn found her footing and walked away from the bar. She needed to find Jennifer and Cassidy. She pulled her phone out of her pocket to text them, then groaned. She had never asked Jennifer about charging her phone. Now it wouldn't turn on.

As she shoved her phone back into her pocket, Caitlyn bumped into a tall furry beast.

Of course there were furries at The Way Station.

Why not?

Except—no; not a furry. Just another regular person.

Feeling light-headed, Caitlyn excused herself and kept walking until someone caught her elbow and guided her toward the stairs leading to the VIP section. Heady excitement overrode her initial alarm. Hadn't she seen Anne Marie there earlier? Maybe the actress could help her find Jennifer and Cassidy. If nothing else, maybe Caitlyn could find her friends more easily from a better vantage point. She didn't even protest when the stranger grasping her elbow wrapped their other arm around her waist.

That was when Spiky Dog Collar Man appeared in front of her, blocking access to the stairs. Caitlyn hadn't appreciated just how tall and expansive he was from across the dance floor before. His open leather vest revealed rippling muscles. Even his quadriceps visibly strained against his leather pant legs. He never skipped arms *or* leg day, that was for sure.

Time in the sun?

That was clearly another matter.

"I'm not letting you take her," he said to the stranger grasping Caitlyn's arm and waist. His voice sounded gruff yet regal.

"If the Lady's got a problem with it, she can come stop it herself instead of sending another one of her guard dogs."

Caitlyn recognized the voice of her bartender. She felt herself starting to swoon and tried to turn around to look at him. "What did you give me?"

ten

. . .

E ither the men (or whatever they were) didn't hear Caitlyn's question, or they were ignoring her as their standoff continued. She fought back her nausea and forced herself to focus on the angry blue-tinged face of Spiky Dog Collar Man in front of her. "We've been drawing too much attention to ourselves," he was saying. "And we're not the only ones here. Just look around. It's only going to get worse."

"Oh, bullshit," the bartender said, letting go of Caitlyn's elbow to caress her arm. "Besides, what's another missing girl in a city like this? We could drop the illusions entirely, and these people would just see what they want to see, anyway. As long as the trains run on time and their stocks are up, that's all anyone here cares about."

Spiky Dog Collar Man took another step forward. "It's not all I care about."

When the bartender's grip loosened even more, Caitlyn pivoted and elbowed him in the stomach. Then she turned around to grasp his shoulders. Caitlyn was about to knee him in the groin when a blond man in a black suit came up from behind and clasped a dark metal collar around the bartender's neck. The bartender clawed at his throat, howling, as his skin appeared to smoke beneath the manacle. The man in black nodded, not at Caitlyn but at Spiky Dog Collar Man behind her, and led the bartender away.

"Hey, I know you!" Caitlyn shouted. She tried to follow but swayed. "I know him!" She glanced at Spiky Dog Collar Man. "I mean, I don't *know him* know him, but I've seen him." She started to follow the man in black. "I've seen you!"

Caitlyn squeaked as she felt herself being lifted. *Man, nobody here pays attention to anything.* Spiky Dog Collar Man carried her out of the club like she weighed next to nothing. "My friends are still in there," Caitlyn told Spiky Dog Collar Man when he set her down on a bench inside.

"Some friends. Is there anyone else you can call to take you home?"

"What if I don't want to go home?" Caitlyn tried to stand but wobbled. She sat back down, glaring up at Spiky Dog Collar Man. "My phone's dead anyway."

Spiky Dog Collar Man sighed. He pulled a phone out of his own pocket. "Here."

Caitlyn's scowl deepened as she grudgingly accepted his phone. She thought for a minute before she remembered Tyler's number. At least she hoped it was his number. It could be the pizza delivery guy for all she could tell in her present state, but they had cars, too, didn't they?

It's Caitlyn. Things got weird. Please come get me? is what she meant to text to Tyler, but not what she typed. She groaned as she fought off another wave of nausea.

"I wish there was something I could give you to make this easier, but I'm afraid the only cure is a good night's sleep," Spiky Dog Collar Man told her. "Maybe I should stay close until your friends get here."

Caitlyn gazed up at him, her eyes coming to rest on his collar. "I'm not so sure that's a good idea. They might not be as cool about some things. Not like I am," she slurred.

"You're looking a little pale." He knelt in front of her.

"Yeah?! Well, you're practically transparent, buddy." Caitlyn started to gesture at his face but became distracted by her fingers. "Should consider taking a bus to Coney Island, catch some rays. The veins. It's creepy, man."

Spiky Dog Collar man rose. "I'm just a scream away if anything happens," he said.

Caitlyn gave him a mock salute as he walked back into the club.

"Who the hell is Ting, and why do I care if they have a wire?"

Max rolled his eyes. "Caitlyn's obviously drunk, Ty. I dunno what happened to Jennifer and Cassidy, or why she's using someone else's phone, but she needs help." He pulled his hoodie off a hook by the door. Tyler followed him out of the apartment, and they flagged down the first taxi they saw.

"The Way Station," Max told the driver, an attractive woman in a ball cap with a blond ponytail.

"You've got the right look," the driver said, looking at Max in the rearview window, "but I dunno if those clothes are up to snuff. And your friend, well…"

"We're not going in," Tyler said. "We're picking up a friend. And we can't all be as good-looking as you," he added. "How many auditions did you tank before you ended up stuck behind the wheel of a cab, anyway?"

"Dude…"

"She started it," Tyler mumbled.

"There she is," Max said several minutes later. "Down that side alley." He pointed.

"Seriously?" The driver pulled up to the curb. She adjusted her ball cap and followed Max and Tyler to where Caitlyn sat on a bench. "These boys say you're their roommate. That true? I don't want them taking advantage of you."

"These nerds?" Caitlyn snorted. "Perfect gentlemen."

"Caitlyn! There you are. We've been looking all over for you." Max and Tyler turned to see Jennifer and Cassidy running down the alley to join them.

"How did you get separated in the first place?" Max glared. "Don't you have each other's numbers?"

Jennifer frowned. "I tried messaging."

"I even called," Cassidy said.

"It was my bad," Caitlyn said. "Battery died."

Max sighed. "Of course it did."

Cassidy sat down next to Caitlyn on the bench. "Are you okay?" She brushed hair back from Caitlyn's face and tucked it behind her ear.

"I can bring your stuff tomorrow." Jennifer sat on the other side of Caitlyn. She took her hand and squeezed. "I'm so sorry we left you at the bar."

"Meter's running." The driver stood with her hands on her waist, looking bored and disinterested.

Caitlyn wrapped her arms around her stomach while a concerned Jennifer rubbed her back. "I don't feel so good," she told Max and Tyler.

"There's an extra charge if she yacks," the driver said.

The three of them got into the back seat, Caitlyn wedged between Max and Tyler. "Well, that was a nightmare and a half. At least I was right about the puppy," she said.

"What puppy?" Tyler looked at Max over the top of Caitlyn's head. Max shrugged.

When they arrived home, Caitlyn barely made it into the bathroom before the heaving started. She didn't even have time to close the door. She sensed someone kneeling beside her as soft hands pulled her hair back from her face.

"I'll take the couch," Caitlyn heard Max say from somewhere far away. "She can have my bunk. Assuming anyone gets any sleep tonight."

"Nah, take my bunk," Tyler said, sounding much closer.

The last thing Caitlyn remembered was the gentle touch of his hand on her back.

eleven

. . .

"How you feeling?" Caitlyn sat up in the bottom bunk as Max walked into the room in a tee shirt and flannel boxers, holding a box of donuts.

"Better. I think. Embarrassed mostly. I saw all sorts of wild shit last night." She looked at the floor where Tyler was sleeping, his face buried into a pillow. She fought the urge to reach down and touch his messy brown hair.

"Yeah, it seemed like you were tripping pretty hard." Max looked concerned.

"I don't suppose the part where Tyler was holding my hair back while I vomited was just another hallucination?"

"No," Max said, "that actually happened. Donut?" He held the box out to Caitlyn.

She considered, then reached for a chocolate donut with sprinkles. "I'm feeling weirdly hungry, all things considered."

"Are you getting crumbs in the bed?" Tyler pushed himself up, sitting with his legs crossed under his blanket as he looked at Caitlyn.

"Like you'd kick her out over it." Max held the box out to Tyler.

"It's your bunk anyway." Tyler took a bite out of his chocolate log. "What happened?"

"Someone drugged me," Caitlyn said.

"Did you set your drink down?"

Caitlyn made a face. "I'm not stupid," she told Max. "It was the bartender." She tried to explain how everyone started looking funny, like they weren't even real people, and how the bartender tried to take her upstairs but then some nice biker guy stopped him. "Then they started arguing about all this stuff, and I have no idea what any of it meant. Oh! Maybe the club is a front for running drugs."

"Maybe." Max looked doubtful.

"And here's the weird part," Caitlyn said. "I think I saw Anne Marie."

"Yeah," Tyler interrupted, "*that's* the weird part."

Caitlyn rolled her eyes. "Not that—she was there with this couple. I think it might have been Elliot and Leanne. That's weird, right? I know she's been spending a lot of time with Leanne and all, but..." She trailed off, cringing.

"Was this before or after you were drugged?"

Caitlyn looked at Max, trying to remember. "Before. I think..."

"Well, it's a little icky and problematic, but it's hardly a crime," Tyler said.

"I'm not so sure about that, like if she's being pressured into doing something to keep her role," Max said, "but it also isn't fair to jump to any conclusions, not when Caitlyn can't even be sure who or what she saw."

"It was definitely Anne Marie," Caitlyn said. "And I'm, like, ninety-five percent sure it was them. But you're right. We shouldn't jump to any conclusions."

Her phone beeped, and she yelped in surprise. It was a text from Christopher. "I almost forgot. I have a date tonight. How wrecked do I look?" she asked Tyler. "You can tell me the truth."

He started to answer, then closed his mouth. "You look beautiful," he said after a moment. "You always look beautiful."

Caitlyn felt her cheeks flush and gave him a small smile even though she knew he only said it to be kind.

"Well, she'll look even better after she showers and runs a comb through that rat's nest. It's not the worst look," Max said. "We just don't want Chris to think you had more fun last night than you actually did."

———

Jennifer and Cassidy stopped by the apartment in the afternoon. "I'm so, so sorry about last night," Jennifer said. "Next time you come out with us, we'll make sure your phone is charged while we're getting ready. And we'll do a better job of sticking together in the first place. I feel so bad we left you sitting at the bar by yourself."

"Have you really been crashing on the couch?" Cassidy gazed at the apartment. "You know, our roommate has been talking about moving back home. Our rent's a little higher, I think, but maybe you could move in with us. Oh, I brought you something." She handed Caitlyn a floral dress on a hanger. "For your date."

Caitlyn ran her hand over the fabric. It was a soft creamy dress with pink and yellow flowers. "Thanks," she said.

"I reminded her you don't like skirts," Jennifer said, "but she insisted on a dress."

"It's perfect," Caitlyn said. "I was only half-serious about the skirts."

When Caitlyn put on the dress, it stopped just past her knees. She did a little twirl in front of the bathroom mirror. Even the sleeves had a little flounce to them. Maybe they could finish the evening with a musical number at the site of her first unofficial date with Christopher. And then a bluebird could land on her finger to join her in song and someone could shoot an arrow through her forehead for being such a ridiculous cheeseball.

"Whatcha thinkin' about?"

Caitlyn jumped, then met Tyler's eyes in the bathroom mirror as he stood behind her with an amused smile. "Mayhem and murder," she said, grateful not for the first time that he couldn't hear her thoughts.

"That's what I figured," he said. "Women only ever get that glow when they think about burying their enemies six feet under."

"You know it!" Caitlyn grinned as she brushed her hair.

Tyler's smile faltered for a moment. "Take care of yourself tonight. Text a pukey face if Chris is boring or lame. I'll make an excuse to get you out of it."

"What's Max doing tonight?"

"He has a date. Some stage manager at another theater. I forget her name. He's got a strict policy about dating anyone he works with."

"After all the drama between Anne Marie and Nick, I get it," Caitlyn said. "I'm sure Chris will be cool no matter what, but I'll definitely text if he decides to be uncool." She turned to smile at Tyler, but he was already wandering back to the couch. He sat down with his laptop and started to watch something online. Whatever it was must have been funny because he started to laugh. He always looked so cute, the way his eyes lit up when he laughed.

No. Bad Caitlyn.

Dating a coworker was pushing it. A roommate? Definitely off limits. Jennifer and Cassidy didn't count because she knew they were a couple before they moved in together. And they didn't share a room with the third.

Someone knocked on the door. Caitlyn glanced at Tyler one last time before opening the door to greet Christopher.

"Are you okay?" Christopher asked. "You seem…distracted."

"What?" Caitlyn looked up from her virgin mojito. "I'm sorry. Just trying to figure out what I'm in the mood to eat, that's all." They sat at a table for two on a balcony overlooking the rest of the restaurant. Below, people engaged in animated conversation with their friends and coworkers around the bar or in booths. The upstairs felt more intimate, apart from the occasional peel of giggles from a rowdy booth of women at a bachelorette party down below.

Christopher leaned back in his chair, looking handsome and relaxed in jeans and a white dress shirt with rolled sleeves. "I've heard the Baja shrimp tacos are good, but the croqueta del mar sounds interesting." He set the menu down on the table and gazed at Caitlyn. "So, how was your girls' night out?"

"Jen and Cass are fun, but The Way Station was…" Caitlyn paused, trying to decide how much to tell him. "It was a little too chaotic."

"Chaotic how?"

Caitlyn shrugged. "The whole night was kind of a blur, to be honest."

"Hmm," Christopher said. "Evasive."

Caitlyn decided to change the subject after the waitress took their orders. "So, how did you spend your Friday night?"

Christopher smirked. "It was a wild night with Matt and Steve and Jack while they played some online shooter and yelled at each other over their headsets."

"Wow," Caitlyn said. "They must have a big apartment."

"Oh yeah," Chris said. "I almost have to straighten my arms to reach either side of the room I'm sharing with Matt. I know I shouldn't complain when I'm lucky he needed a roommate, but do you have any idea what it's like bunking with someone who talks in their sleep? I almost hit the deck at three in the morning because he started yelling about another squad coming in hot. Or maybe he was still up playing his game. Who's to say?"

"I'd invite you to share the couch with me, but then we'd be right on top of…" Caitlyn felt her eyes widen. "A sentence I'm not going to finish." Another scream of laughter down below as if the bachelorette party overheard their conversation.

"And I'm going to pretend the sentence never even started. Because I'm a gentleman." Christopher's eyes twinkled as he leaned forward in his seat. Caitlyn was about to tell him that he didn't need to be when the waitress returned with their food. The conversation moved on to their families and childhood, with Caitlyn giving Christopher the broad strokes about hers while he shared one funny anecdote after another.

Afterward, Christopher walked her back to the apartment. "I had a really nice time tonight," Caitlyn said at the door. He had insisted on coming all the way up with her, so she was surprised when he only kissed her on the cheek.

"See you Monday," he said, giving her one last grin before leaving. Caitlyn pursed her lips in disappointment as she watched him turn and walk down the stairs.

Tyler looked up from his laptop when Caitlyn walked into the apartment. "It's not even ten o'clock." He checked the time and raised an eyebrow. "Kind of an early night, but I guess he never got lame or boring?"

"I think I might have been the lame, boring one," Caitlyn said, sitting down beside him on the couch. She wrapped her blanket around herself before resting her head against his shoulder.

"Catie, you are many things, but you could never be lame or boring." Tyler adjusted, putting an arm around her shoulder. Then he kissed the top of her head.

Caitlyn sensed the entire length of his body tense in horror at the impulsive move. "What are we watching?" she asked before he could freak out completely.

Tyler relaxed. "Well, I was watching funny animal videos. But somehow, I ended up on a documentary about the domestication of wolves. I still don't get how we went from wolves to little yappy ankle biter dogs, though."

"Right?" Caitlyn settled in beside him as he started the video back up.

Max came home from his date to find Caitlyn and Tyler leaning against each other and asleep on the couch—Caitlyn still dressed from her night out. He considered waking them, but carefully removed the laptop from Tyler's lap instead and closed the lid.

twelve

. . .

Caitlyn felt uneasy as she walked to the theater with Max and Tyler the following Monday, but she could not pinpoint why. She had untangled herself from Tyler Sunday morning while he was still asleep, and nobody had said anything about it or acted as though anything were weird or different, so it wasn't that. Christopher had sent a nice text message. She even had a conversation with Jennifer and Cassidy. It was all good in the hood, she told herself…

…so why did she feel this nagging trepidation?

"Has anyone seen Anne Marie?" Everyone looked up as Sophia came into the dressing room. "She's usually here by now."

Elise was keeping to herself in a corner, braiding her hair. She shrugged. "I haven't talked to her since last week. Have you tried Leanne's dressing room? They're probably hanging out in there."

"Pass," Sophia said, cringing. She set her gym bag down.

Maya was watching their exchange, smirking. She caught Caitlyn's eyes in the dressing room mirror and raised her eyebrows.

She must know something, but what? Caitlyn thought.

"Did you have fun this weekend?"

"What?" Caitlyn looked over at Laurel. "Oh, yeah." She decided not to tell Laurel about what happened at The Way Station. "Jen and

Cass are great. Then I went out with Chris on Saturday. That went well…I think. Did you do anything fun?"

"I talked to someone, a little, but mostly I just practiced," Laurel said, her cheeks reddening. She turned to leave the dressing room.

Did Matt take time from his gaming to message Laurel? Caitlyn considered the possibility as she walked after Laurel into the green room. Most of the men were already inside practicing a group number, except for the three chorus men, who would be sailors during this scene.

"Risers will be set backstage for this scene with microphones placed to pick up your voices," Diane explained once everyone had gathered. Everyone but Anne Marie. "Now, there aren't any words, but it's important that everyone stays together and in tune for this piece."

At first, Caitlyn felt silly oohing and aahing, but once everyone learned their individual parts and they began practicing the piece together, she had no problem envisioning Dracula tormenting the doomed sailors. As the eerie melody built up to a frenzy, Caitlyn felt goosebumps raise on her arms.

This was good. This was very good.

"This is a mess," Sophia complained when they broke for lunch. "Anne Marie's missing. Elise has barely said one word to me…where'd she go, anyway?" She looked up and down the hall while she filled her plate with finger sandwiches and chips.

"Probably snuck into one of the dressing rooms with Nick," Maya said.

Emma giggled, and Amelia bit her lip on a smile. Christopher ignored the whole exchange and walked away with his food. Caitlyn wanted to go with him, but he appeared to be joining some of the other men in their dressing room.

"What are you talking about?" Sophia stared at Maya.

"Like you didn't know," Emma said. "That's why Anne Marie got so upset on Friday."

"And why she's not here today," Maya said.

Sophia shook her head. "It's not like Anne Marie to miss rehearsal." Her frown deepened. "Especially over some stupid boy."

And Nick is stupider than most.

Now Caitlyn frowned. Maybe Anne Marie's absence had nothing to do with Nicholas at all. She thought of the blonde she saw heading up the stairs to the VIP section at The Way Station. Maybe that's what the men were arguing about—not drug running, but human trafficking. She felt a chill at remembering how close she may have come to that same fate. And though Caitlyn didn't like Anne Marie all that much, she liked the thought of her coming to harm even less. She hoped she was wrong, and Anne Marie really was just sulking at home.

Tyler stood waiting in the audience as Elliot approached the choreography on stage.

"Has anyone heard anything?" Isabella asked, her brow knitted together.

"Still MIA." Elliot shrugged. "Why don't you work with the brides on one of their numbers, and Diane can work on something else with the other cast members," he said. "Something we don't need Lucy for?"

Isabella's worry lines deepened. "Michael is running lines with Leanne, and Andre isn't even scheduled to come in today. There's not a lot more to work on without them. And some people are still struggling with the quickstep. Fortunately, Anne Marie is not one of them."

"So put one of the other girls back in, and someone who already knows the choreography can fill in for Anne Marie," Elliot said. "If she's a no-call/no-show again tomorrow, she's out."

Isabella nodded. "Cue the ballroom scene music," she told Tyler.

He nodded and walked back to the sound booth.

———

"Caitlyn, I need you to dance with Anne Marie's partners today," Isabella said as the cast came on stage. She did not say anything about

Anne Marie but Caitlyn noticed her smile did not reach her eyes. Concern tempered her own enthusiasm. "Nick, try not to mangle another performer's feet today. Sophia, I need you to take Caitlyn's place, just for today."

Sophia looked ill. Elise glared.

"See you later, partner," Christopher said. He tipped the brim of an imaginary hat.

Caitlyn gave him a sad smile, but deep down she felt elated to be singled out by Isabella—even if it did mean more dancing with Nicholas. For his part, the actor appeared humbled by Isabella's criticism and behaved well enough, even if he did stumble a few times during the quickstep.

"I bet you're a shoo-in if Anne Marie doesn't come back," Jennifer said after rehearsal. Cassidy nodded in agreement.

Caitlyn felt a shiver of anticipation run up and down her spine. Then guilt crept in and settled in the pit of her stomach. She left the dressing room to join Max and Tyler in the hall. "I know we're all thinking the same thing," she said to them.

"Which is…?" Tyler looked from Caitlyn to Max.

"*Outside*," she said with a furtive glance down either side of the hallway.

"It was Anne Marie that I saw at the club on Friday, and someone kidnapped her…or worse," Caitlyn said once they were walking away from the building. "We should notify the police or something…right?"

"And tell them what?" Tyler asked, stopping.

Max touched Caitlyn's shoulder. "Caitlyn, you're not even sure what you saw. As soon as the police hear you were drugged, well, that's not a can of worms I think you wanna open. And they won't take anything you say seriously after that."

"But…"

"Look, we all care about Anne Marie…we all care if something happened to Anne Marie," Max amended after Tyler raised an eyebrow, "Because we're human and she's human, probably, and we'd be assholes if we didn't, but I don't think there's anything we can do here."

Caitlyn deflated. "You're right."

"It's good that you care," Tyler said, offering Caitlyn a smile. "Anne Marie would be lucky to have a friend like you."

That just made Caitlyn feel worse. As far as she could tell, nobody else seemed to care much at all, except maybe Sophia. Anne Marie wasn't the nicest person, but she was still a person. Caitlyn could only hope she was okay.

thirteen

. . .

Caitlyn was walking by the main office the following morning when she heard her name. She tried not to listen in, but the temptation was too great. "But Caitlyn already knows the most challenging dances. It's just a matter of adjusting partners," she heard Isabella say, and her heart sped up.

"The producers wanted someone with more star power in the role of Lucy," Elliot said. "It should have been Maya all along. I don't know what I was thinking. Anne Marie was clearly a mistake."

"Maya *is* a quick study," Isabella said. "I'm sure she'll make a wonderful Lucy."

Caitlyn continued past the door, wishing she hadn't snooped.

Elliot and Isabella stood in the green room beside Diane. Most of the cast sat in rows of chairs in front of them. Caitlyn sat down behind Jennifer and Cassidy, next to Laurel. Jennifer looked back at her with an excited grin, and Caitlyn forced herself to smile back.

"As you've probably noticed," Elliot began, "we're down a cast member. You may remember Hailey Williams from auditions. She is joining the chorus." He nodded at a woman with glossy jet black curls in the front row. "Which brings me to the role of Lucy."

Caitlyn tried to ignore it as other performers glanced in her direction.

"I know it's going to be a bit of a transition, but we're still very early in the workshopping process, and Maya has assured me she's more than up to the challenge of taking on the role of Lucy."

Though Elliot was only confirming what Caitlyn already knew, she felt numb with disappointment anyway. Hopefully, he didn't have anything important to say, because she spaced out during the rest of the meeting. When people started congratulating her as he finished speaking, she stared at them in confusion.

"Sucks we won't spend as much time together, but I'm so excited for you," Cassidy said.

"You'll be great," Jennifer said.

Emma and Amelia were hovering patiently. If Maya was recast as Lucy, someone needed to replace her as one of Dracula's brides. Caitlyn realized that someone must be her.

"Time to meet Andre. Finally! Isabella is teaching us the routine to 'The Children of the Night,'" Emma said. "I can't wait. I think he's one of my favorite Phantoms, but I loved him in *Rock of Ages*, too," she gushed.

Caitlyn followed them out of the green room to the stage in a daze while the rest of the crew stayed behind to work with Diane on the songs for the ballroom scene.

Emma just about swooned when they walked on stage. When she grabbed at Caitlyn's arm, Caitlyn worried Emma might take her down with her. She followed Emma's gaze to the stage where Andre stood with Isabella. He was dressed simply in a cream sweater and loose gray pants, glasses perched on the end of his nose as he gazed down at the script in his hands. Despite hints of silver at his temples, his face was unlined and chiseled.

"I say 'Listen to them, the children of the night…what music they make,' and then the song begins," Andre said, slipping in and out of the distinctive intonations expected of the dark prince and his own soft eastern European accent. "It's a bit…" He paused as he searched for the right word. "Cheesy, isn't it?"

"I'm told it's an improvement from the last attempt," Isabella said. "We're still workshopping. I'm sure Elliot will value any feedback you have to give." She turned to look at the control booth. "Tyler, do you have the music cued? I want everyone to listen to get a sense of the tempo before we start working through the choreography."

Caitlyn waved up at the control booth with a rueful grin, just in case Max or Tyler were looking. The music began with a gentle piano melody.

"This doesn't at all sound like a knock-off of a similarly named song in Andre's repertoire," Amelia muttered as the strings kicked in.

"It's not like we're making another rock opera," Emma whispered back. "It's fine."

As if responding to their conversation, the music transitioned into a cacophony of creepier sounds, including cymbals and kettledrums. Emma gave Amelia a look as if to say, "I told you so."

"Alright then, let's begin." Andre removed his sweater. Underneath he wore a black tank top, revealing muscular arms and a slender physique.

"Try not to faint," Amelia said, giving Emma a pat on the back as she watched Andre drape his sweater over a chair offstage. She turned to Caitlyn. "Ready to collaborate with a Broadway star?"

Emma behaved herself during rehearsal, but Andre was all she could talk about during lunch as they sat around the dressing room. "Obviously you can sense how magnetic he is from the audience. He wouldn't be a star otherwise, but working with him, it's on a whole other level. And it's all about the art. He's very generous to his fellow performers. It's not about his ego at all."

"What about Matthew?" Maya asked, exchanging a knowing smile with Amelia.

Caitlyn glanced at Laurel, who stiffened.

"What about him?" Emma asked. "I guess he's fine, for a relative newcomer, I haven't really worked with him, but I feel like I'm learning so much from Andre already. You'll understand when you get to perform with him."

"We begin working on our scenes later this week," Maya said. "I think an intimacy coach is coming in, too."

"I've no doubt he'll be a consummate professional," Emma said smugly.

Caitlyn returned to the dressing room after working on the vocals for "The Children of the Night" with Diane. Laurel was sitting at one of the sinks, cleaning makeup off her face. "I always feel so energized when I'm on stage," Laurel confided. "The rest of it, like all the backstage type stuff, I dunno…do you ever feel completely drained by the time you go home?"

Caitlyn thought about it. "Some people leave me feeling more drained than others," she said. Deep down, Caitlyn suspected other people felt the same way about her. Her former roommates came to mind. She considered the possibility that people could be bad fits for each other without being bad on an individual basis.

"It's nice talking to someone who understands," Laurel said.

Caitlyn realized this was one of their longer conversations. Laurel didn't open up very often. "I like going for walks on the weekend," she said. "Helps me clear my head. Maybe you could join me sometime. I'd love to have the company."

"Or you could stay with me on Staten Island," Laurel said. "I'm sure my parents wouldn't mind."

Caitlyn smiled, pleased at the invitation.

"So, you're having a good day," Max said when Caitlyn walked outside after rehearsal. He was leaning against the wall of the theater, but when he saw her, he straightened. Tyler stood beside him, hands shoved in his pockets.

"I made a new friend!" Caitlyn grinned at him.

"Andre?" Tyler raised an eyebrow.

Caitlyn tilted her head, puzzled. "No, Laurel. Oh!" She smacked her forehead. "You mean because I'm one of Dracula's brides now. Oh." Her eyes widened. "Oh wow. I just remembered—that means bonus pay, too!" She squealed and hugged Tyler, then Max.

"I like it when Caitlyn has good days," Tyler said to Max.

fourteen

. . .

Caitlyn realized she hadn't called her father since she made the show. "I hope I'm not getting your voicemail because you're afraid I'm asking for more money. Guess what? I don't need it! I made the show. In between apartments right now, but it's cool. Love ya, bye!"

Tyler picked something up off the floor near Caitlyn's duffle bag. He looked back and forth from the picture to Caitlyn's face. "This your family?" He held out the picture. "You have your mom's eyes."

"Thanks." Caitlyn took the photo and slipped it back into her bag. "So, what does everyone want for dinner tonight?" She looked at Max and Tyler with a wide smile. "My treat! I know this great sushi place."

Tyler grinned.

"Are you sure?" Max asked.

"Why not?" Caitlyn asked, defiant. She'd caught the look he gave Tyler. "It's the least I can do after everything you've done for me," she added, softening her tone. "Come on." She turned to walk to the door before Max could argue.

"Any room for dessert?"

"Absolutely," Caitlyn answered. She couldn't help but remember the last time she ate here was the day she'd hit rock bottom. Now things were finally starting to look up, even if she was still crashing on a couch instead of living in an apartment of her own. "You have to share the fried ice cream with me," she told Max and Tyler. "Green tea. It's the best. We're celebrating," she told their waitress. "I'm workshopping this new Broadway musical, about Dracula? At first, I was just in the chorus, but now I'm one of his brides."

"I've heard about that," the waitress said. Her dark hair was pulled back in a fashionably messy bun, and she looked like she was about their age. Her name tag read Carrie. "That's Elliot Dunn's new show, right?" Her lips twitched in the corner when she said his name, like she just saw something gross skitter across the floor on six legs.

Max must have caught the look, too. "You know him?"

"We were in a playwriting class together at NYU. My major's English lit, but I'm thinking of minoring in drama. He seemed nice enough when he hit it big with *A Knight in Brooklyn*. Quiet. Didn't let it go to his head." Carrie tucked a stray strand of hair behind her ear, looking pensive. "Then he met someone new, and...I dunno, something changed. Or maybe he was always that way, and I didn't notice...Anyway, I'm sure the musical will be great. It sounds really exciting."

"I get the impression she was more than just classmates with Elliot," Tyler said after Carrie had gone to put their dessert order in.

"Explains why she's not a fan now," Max said.

"Well, if they were dating or whatever and he blew her off for someone else, it makes sense." Caitlyn stifled a frown. She wondered about the director. Not for the first time, the memory of a familiar blonde following a couple up the stairs at The Way Station replayed itself. She forced the thought away when Carrie returned with their fried ice cream.

Maya appeared to take over Anne Marie's dressing room, but she did not spend a lot of time around Leanne as Anne Marie had. "That girl gives me the creeps," she said one day when she came into the larger dressing room after rehearsal.

Amelia gave her a sympathetic smile. "How are things going, otherwise?"

"Andre really is wonderful to work with," Maya said, ignoring Emma, who glared at her reflection in the mirror. "And Nick only stepped on my foot once during the quickstep yesterday. But Elliot's a bit of a tyrant, and I don't know where Leanne's head is half the time. Don't get me wrong, she never misses a cue, and she knows all her lines—until Elliot changes them—but I dunno. It feels like she's just going through the motions."

"Walking through the…," Laurel started to sing in her soft but sweet voice before she noticed everyone turning to stare. She trailed off, looking down at the floor.

Caitlyn remembered the waitress from the other night. "It must be hard," she said. "Working with someone you're dating. Especially someone as demanding as Elliot." She frowned, feeling uneasy. "But we probably shouldn't be talking about it. It's not appropriate."

"Talking about it, or the relationship itself?" Amelia asked.

"That's why I like to keep business and pleasure separate." This time Maya did acknowledge Emma, giving her a pointed look as she said, "Office romances are messy, even if you're on somewhat equal footing. Just look at what happened to Anne Marie."

"What *did* happen to Anne Marie?" Sophia glanced at Elise, whose cheeks flushed. "It's like she dropped off the face of the earth. I refuse to believe this is all about stupid Nick. He is *not* all that, and Anne Marie would never let some dumbass boy come between her and her dreams. Something bad happened, I know it."

The other women shrugged.

What's another missing girl in a city like this?

Caitlyn's uneasiness grew. Where had she heard that before?

fifteen

. . .

Tyler stood on the catwalk helping Max gel some lights Friday morning. "When do Billy and Jordan start coming in?"

"Next week. I think the wardrobe department will be here, too, to start fittings."

Tyler stared down at the stack of gels in his hand. "You know," he said, "I feel kind of bad for Amber. Do you think she has daddy issues? Seriously, though, who comes up with some of these awful gel names?"

"She's going to therapy, it's fine." Max rolled his eyes, then turned to give Tyler a dirty look. "Wait. You didn't bring up more of the bastard amber, did you? That's what's already in there. Elliot wanted something redder for the ballroom scene. He still wants it soft and pretty, but he also wants to hint at the danger to come. That's why I wanted to try the rose gold."

"Oh, right," Tyler said. "I think I remembered your directions backwards."

"Did you take your meds before we left?"

Tyler glared. "Yes." Then he stopped to think. "No. No, I did not. I remember. I was reaching for the bottle, but then Caitlyn needed the bathroom, and I forgot. She always looks so cute when her eyes get all big and…"

Max raised an eyebrow.

"I'll go back down for the rose gold."

"Coming with," Max said. "To make sure you don't get mixed up again."

"Uh huh."

Max and Tyler paused at the bottom of the stairs when they heard voices.

"She left in a huff last Friday," Elliot was saying as he led a couple of uniformed police officers backstage. "Haven't seen or heard from her since. It was really unprofessional of her," he added. "At least we're early enough in the process that it wasn't a problem recasting her role. These girls. Sometimes the pressure is too much for them."

"Mmhmm," said one of the police officers. She sounded unimpressed.

"Well, if you remember anything that can help—"began the other officer.

"I know where to reach you," Elliot finished smoothly. "Sorry, I couldn't be of more—"

"We'd still like to speak with other members of the cast and crew," the first officer interrupted, her tone even but commanding. Elliot and the police officers now stood where Tyler could see them, even though darkness concealed him from view. "Maybe they have more information that can help us pin down a timeline for Anne Marie's disappearance."

Elliot's brow furrowed for a moment, but he offered a quick smile. "Of course," he said, opening the door leading to the hallway.

Tyler turned to look at Max. "Well, if Elliot and Leanne were with Anne Marie at the club, he's not saying so. Do you think Caitlyn will tell them what she saw?"

"Dunno." Max frowned. "But I wonder if we should have taken her more seriously."

• • •

"Well, that was awkward," Caitlyn said, walking out of the dressing room after talking to a female officer. She'd mentioned the possibility of seeing Anne Marie at the Way Station but left Leanne and Elliot out of it.

"Right?" Christopher stepped into the hall from the men's dressing room. "I'm gonna see if Isabella's ready for me on stage. I miss my favorite dance partner," he added, tipping the brim of his invisible hat before he turned to walk away. Caitlyn watched him go. With a twinge of disappointment, she realized it was the first time they'd really spoken to each other all week. Maya's words about office romance came back to her. It was probably for the best.

"At last, my final bride arrives," Andre said in his Dracula voice, stretching his arms wide as Caitlyn walked into the green room. "We can begin."

She gave him an accommodating grin. For a Broadway star, Andre was down to earth, and even a bit of a nerd. Caitlyn found it comforting, somehow. And it was funny when American words or idioms confused him, even though she suspected it was in jest. "Always with this breaking of the legs," he'd tease. "What is it with you Americans, wishing harm upon your fellow actors?"

The wink was a dead giveaway.

Tyler passed Elliot and Leanne speaking in hushed voices on his way to the control booth after lunch. He could not make out anything they were saying, but Leanne appeared even paler than usual, and Elliot's face was stern as he spoke to her with a hand on her shoulder.

As he reached the door, a bark of laughter caught Tyler's attention. He glanced at the stage, where Caitlyn stood listening to Andre. The distinguished older man briefly touched her elbow before moving across the stage.

Tyler scowled as he opened the door and stepped inside. "Why do all actors have to be so damn handsome?"

Max looked up. "Yeah, nobody makes me weak in the knees like Lloyd does," he deadpanned. "The way he slurps up those gummy worms every time I pass him in the hall. It's all I can do to keep my hands to myself."

"Method actors. Blech." Tyler slumped down in his chair in front of the sound booth. "It's easy for you," he told Max. "You're one of the beautiful people. You don't know what it's like having to compensate for average looks with a great personality and funny jokes. What chance do guys like me have when guys that look like that get to be clever and talented, too?"

"Dude," Max said. "I'm not just prettier than you. I'm funnier, too. Get back to work."

———

"So, what did you tell them?"

Caitlyn didn't answer Max right away as they left the theater. She sensed someone staring and turned to look. Lloyd slouched against the wall outside the theater beside the back door, his wild brown hair sticking this way and that. She made the mistake of making eye contact just as he sucked up a gummy worm. Caitlyn closed her eyes, cringing. She turned back to Max and Tyler. "Uhm. Not much. I mentioned seeing someone I thought might be her at The Way Station. She wrote it down." Caitlyn shrugged. "Seemed wrong to include Elliot and Leanne when I can't be sure what I saw."

"I guess they'll be investigating there next," Tyler said.

"It's out of our hands now," Max said. "You did what you cou—"

An ear-piercing shriek interrupted him.

All three looked as Lloyd giggled and gave Elise a curtsy and a little wave. She stalked off, pulling a gummy worm out of her hair and muttering profanities under her breath.

Max turned back to Caitlyn and Tyler. "This place is a looney bin."

"I know, Max." Tyler grinned.

sixteen

. . .

"Would you believe Laurel's never been to Coney Island?" Max and Tyler exchanged a look while watching Caitlyn pack a satchel to spend the weekend with Laurel on Staten Island. "I'd believe it," Tyler said.

Max nodded. He turned back to the stove, stirring ramen in a large pot.

"Imagine growing up in New York City without having had a real Coney dog," Caitlyn mused. "I've only been here for like a year, and I think I've already experienced more of the city than Laurel has. It's a wonder her parents let her leave the island to perform."

"Sounds like Laurel could use a change of scenery," Tyler said.

Max poured ramen into a couple of plastic bowls. "Has she considered moving out?"

"I think she has to ease her parents into the idea slowly," Caitlyn said. "Hopefully, I can make a good impression. Show them how mature and responsible I am…are you okay?" She looked at Max in concern as he appeared to choke on a mouthful of ramen. "Don't put so much in your mouth at once," she advised.

"You made sure your phone is charged, right?" Tyler gave Max a napkin before taking another bite of his own ramen.

Caitlyn pouted. "I never make the same mistake twice." She glanced down at her phone. The battery life said sixty-eight percent. *Good enough.* "I gotta hustle if I'm gonna catch the R and get to the ferry in time. Laurel is meeting me at the St. George terminal with her parents." She shouldered her satchel and left the apartment.

Max blew on his steaming bowl. "What's the over/under on Caitlyn winning over Laurel's snotty suburbanite parents?"

"I'm always betting on Caitlyn," Tyler said.

"Even when the chips are down?"

"Especially then."

Caitlyn made it to the ferry just in time. She folded her arms and leaned over the railing as a light breeze blew back her hair. Standing beside her, a little girl with brown hair in braided pigtails pulled at her mother's blouse.

"Mommy, mommy, I see a mermaid. I see a mermaid, mommy!"

"That's nice, sweetie," said the mother, busy looking at something on her phone. "Did you wave 'hello'?"

The little girl looked down over the railing, started to wave, then screamed. "There's something wrong with its eyes," she said, her brown eyes wide as her apologetic mother guided her away from the railing.

Caitlyn looked down at the water and saw nothing but waves, some glistening with sunlight. Kids and their imaginations. She remembered the time she insisted to her own mother that a gremlin lived in the tree outside her bedroom window.

Caitlyn turned away from the water and leaned back against the railing as she watched the other passengers. She had taken the first ferry after rush hour ended, so most passengers were tourists, or small groups and couples. It was a shame she couldn't have taken a later ferry to enjoy the sunset, but Laurel's parents were pushing back dinner as it was.

Laurel stood waiting when the ferry reached the St. George terminal. "Dad didn't want to pay for parking even though it's only a couple of dollars, so he's sorta just driving around the courthouse," she said with a shrug as they walked.

"You do a lot of camping?" Caitlyn asked as a silver Ford Bronco pulled up to the curb. Laurel replied with another shrug as they slid into the back seat of the car.

"Hope you didn't have to wait too long." A middle-aged man with wispy graying blond hair and brown eyes peered at Caitlyn and Laurel in the rearview mirror. "Last time I parked here, someone scratched my car and didn't even leave a note. Must've been somebody from the city."

"Cars were banned from the ferry years ago, dear," said the woman in the passenger seat. Her brown hair was pulled back from her forehead with a headband, and her brown eyes were tired but kind. "I hope you girls are hungry. I have a pot roast cooking at home."

Caitlyn's stomach growled in response. "Sorry," she said.

Laurel's parents chuckled.

"How long's it been since you had a good home-cooked meal?" Mr. Locke asked.

"Uhm, over a year, I think," Caitlyn said in between bites of overcooked pot roast and under seasoned potatoes. *And it will be a while longer still*, she thought. The limp slices of carrot were particularly sad. She pretended not to notice when Laurel deftly deposited some from her plate into the napkin draped across her lap.

Instead, Caitlyn looked around at the pictures on the dining room wall. Laurel in different spangly outfits at dance recitals from five years on, similar to photos of Caitlyn back home. School photos, family photos. Mr. Locke looking boisterous, Mrs. Locke more reserved, and Laurel, awkward and uncomfortable in general. The Lockes lived in a small home with a green lawn and nondescript but elegant décor. Beige walls, taupe furniture, a splash of color from a fake potted plant here or there. It was all so…nice, though it wasn't very cozy.

"Does your mother like to cook?" Mrs. Locke asked.

"She died when I was in high school," Caitlyn said. "Cancer. But Dad always liked to say she could burn toast," she continued before the Lockes could express their condolences. "I guess because she was always burning toast." She gave a rueful smile. "She'd try to make a grilled cheese sandwich or a quesadilla, but then she'd get bored and start cleaning the kitchen or watching something on TV and forget all about it until the fire alarm went off. Dad makes the best spaghetti, though."

Caitlyn could only hope Laurel's parents didn't judge her. Sure, she had a few quirks as the consequence of losing her mother at such a volatile time in her life. But Mrs. Locke gazed at her with pity, and Mr. Locke's piercing gaze made her feel like she was under a microscope. She looked over at Laurel, who attempted a reassuring smile without success.

Laurel's room was not what Caitlyn expected. Oh, the four-poster bed with the billowy pink panels hanging from the canopy seemed about right. But a strange assortment of collectible fairies sat on the bookshelf, not the traditional sort with flowers for hats sitting on toadstools, but edgier fairies with striped leggings and colorful hair, a cat with batlike wings, and other strange and wondrous creatures. It all made Caitlyn breathe a sigh of relief. At least Laurel had a space to be herself in this house. The framed art on the walls mirrored the themes of her collection.

"Dad hates all this stuff," Laurel said, standing behind her.

"I like it," Caitlyn said. "But your dad probably hates me, too."

"I don't think Dad likes anyone, except maybe Mom," Laurel told her. "He just acts nice for his business." Caitlyn stifled a laugh, noting Laurel's serious expression.

"You won't believe how mad he got when I told him we were going to Coney Island tomorrow," Laurel continued. "Mom reminded him I'm an adult now and told him he should probably keep some of his opinions to himself so you don't get the wrong idea about our family. Then he got mad at her, but it's all fine now. Everything's fine." She nodded as if trying to convince herself.

Caitlyn made a mental note to call her own dad again this weekend and thank him for, well, pretty much everything.

seventeen

. . .

"I still don't like this," Mr. Locke said the following morning. "There was another one of those stabbings there just the other week. Helluva lotta good coming down on lawful gun owners has done. It's just like…" He went off on a diatribe about what some caller into his favorite talk radio show had said while Mrs. Locke pressed a couple fingertips to her temple.

Caitlyn decided to ignore him. "We're going to Central Park first," she said to Mrs. Locke. "Then the Metropolitan Museum of Art. After lunch, we'll take the subway to Coney Island." Mr. Locke scoffed when she mentioned the subway, but Caitlyn continued undeterred. "After that it's a short bus ride back to Staten Island, and I guess we'll get a taxi from there or call for a ride if it's not too late to pick us up."

"Sounds like you have everything all planned out," Mrs. Locke said. She gave her husband a pointed look.

"Thanks! I've gotten really good at navigating the city," Caitlyn said.

Laurel hugged her thin hoodie to herself as the wind rustled through the trees.

"I'm sorry. I swear this has never happened to me before." Caitlyn frowned as she turned in a circle. "I know this park like the back of my hand."

"It's okay," Laurel said. "Sometimes I get turned around in the park near my home." She considered telling Caitlyn about the time she stayed until dusk, lost in a book until she noticed the temperature drop and saw strange eyes in the darkening woods, but decided to keep it to herself. Caitlyn seemed so confident and self-assured, and Laurel worried about sounding foolish.

"It's like all my personal landmarks are just picking themselves up and moving around." Caitlyn pulled her phone out of the pocket in her leggings. "That's what I get for going off the path. Even my phone can't tell where we are." She looked up and stared at something behind Laurel, squinting. "Wait a minute."

Laurel turned to see a hulking feline shape through some trees.

She gasped and backed into Caitlyn.

"It's not a real panther," Caitlyn said, laughing. "Just a sculpture." She stepped around Laurel, pushing her way through the foliage. Laurel followed as Caitlyn slid down a small hill to the sidewalk below. A few passersby stared at them, and Caitlyn grinned and waved. They quickened their pace, hurrying away. "Just a few blocks to the museum. It's all good." She plucked a leaf from Laurel's hair.

Laurel looked back at the statue atop the hill. It still looked ready to pounce.

She shivered.

"What's scarier?" Caitlyn asked. "Mummies or vampires?"

"Huh?" Laurel looked away from the statue of a mummified cat. "It feels wrong to be talking about this. Disrespectful." After a beat, she said. "Vampires, I guess. They can suck the life out of you."

"So can mummies! Haven't you seen the movie?"

Laurel shook her head.

"You need to see the movie," Caitlyn told her. "It's the best. It's so funny."

"I thought mummies were supposed to be scary." Laurel followed

Caitlyn to stand in front of a statue of the goddess Isis with her son Horus. "Have you ever noticed how a lot of ancient religions depicted their gods as blue? I always thought that was interesting."

Caitlyn shrugged. "I know movies better than mythology." Something about Laurel's question bothered her, but she couldn't put her finger on what.

Caitlyn discovered Laurel was a fountain of knowledge on world mythologies, Arthurian lore in particular. "But I'm interested in all of it," Laurel was saying as they walked through the gallery of European art and sculpture. "I'm really good at recognizing patterns, and I like seeing how different stories and beliefs travel and transform throughout history."

"I thought King Arthur was real," Caitlyn said.

"That's the tricky part," Laurel said. "The stories are based in history, but I doubt some fairy lady popped out of a lake to present him with a sword. It's all sort of garbled together, history, folklore, mythology…like the world's most epic and long running game of telephone." She grinned. "Turns out Matthew is interested in a lot of the same stuff I am. Except he always relates it back to some computer game."

As they talked, Caitlyn noticed Laurel lit up the same way she did when she was dancing, but she also blushed a little whenever Matthew came up—which was often. Something told Caitlyn she probably shouldn't press the subject. Best to let Laurel open up at her own pace. Instead, she looked back at a painting of a gothic cathedral and asked, "Dracula was based on real stuff, too, wasn't he?"

"Vlad the Impaler," Laurel said.

Laurel was midway through her mini-lecture on Vlad and worldwide vampire lore when Caitlyn's stomach interrupted with a growl. "All this talk about scary blood sucking fiends has made me work up an appetite."

"Gross," Laurel said, but she laughed so loudly that other museumgoers turned to stare. Laurel slapped a hand over her mouth, and Caitlyn dissolved into giggles as well.

· · ·

"That's interesting," Max mused.

"Hmm?" Tyler looked up from his sandwich over at his roommate, who sat on the couch reading something on his laptop.

"They shut down The Way Station. Sounds like Anne Marie isn't the only person to disappear in connection with the club." Max continued to read, eyebrows raised. "A couple were from out of state. Suspicions of drug running, human trafficking. Not even bothering to hide it with a name like 'The Way Station' either. The headlines write themselves. The Feds are getting involved in the investigation."

"Scary stuff," Tyler said. "That could've been Caitlyn."

"Well, at least we can rule out Elliot," Max said, closing his laptop. "Between his education and his blossoming career, Elliot may be an overachiever, but I doubt he can include crime lord on his resume."

"I still don't trust the guy," Tyler said.

eighteen

. . .

A few slices of pizza and two subway rides later, Caitlyn and Laurel arrived at Coney Island. "It's nice having someone to do the silly tourist stuff with," Caitlyn said as they navigated the crowd of people enjoying another unseasonably warm spring day. "And having the money for the silly tourist stuff. When I first moved out last summer, I just played on the beach and walked along the boardwalk."

"By yourself?" Laurel's brown eyes were wide.

"My roommates weren't really into this sort of thing. They're older," Caitlyn said. "Besides, I'm used to being on my own."

Laurel frowned.

"This is better, though," Caitlyn said. "Do you go swimming in the summer?"

"We fly to South Carolina to visit family once a year," Laurel told her, "but my parents don't like the local beaches as much."

"I've heard the Myrtle Beach boardwalk is even better."

"Never been." Laurel shrugged. "My uncle has a lake house we stay at."

"That's cool." Caitlyn slipped off her shoes and held them with one hand as she stepped down into the beach sand. Laurel hesitated, then sat down to unlace her shoes and remove her socks. They walked closer to the water and watched as a few kids splashed in the surf while their parents bemoaned the water temperature.

"A little girl thought she saw a mermaid when I was riding the ferry last night," Caitlyn said.

Laurel giggled. "I liked to pretend I was a mermaid when I was little. So did my cousins. Then we got older and all they cared about was boys and makeup. Except Howie, obviously. I mean, not obviously, but well, you know. He just got grouchy and spent all his time online or hunting with his friends."

"I haven't seen my cousins in years. My mom was an only child like me, and my dad's brother lives on the other side of the country." Caitlyn took a few tentative steps into the water. "The Pacific is way colder. Even in the summer."

Laurel set her shoes down and followed Caitlyn into the water. "I like it when you're standing in the sand and the tide comes in and pulls it all away. It almost feels like you're movi—"

Laurel shrieked mid-sentence as something grabbed at her ankle. She tugged herself free and ran until she was nearly all the way back to the boardwalk.

Caitlyn caught up to her, holding Laurel's tennis shoes in her other hand. "Are you okay? What happened?"

"I felt something," Laurel said. "It grabbed my ankle."

Caitlyn looked doubtful. "Probably just seaweed."

"It wasn't slimy. It was strong. Seaweed doesn't have a grip."

They turned to look back at the water. The kids continued to play, oblivious to whatever danger Laurel sensed. "I'm sorry," she said. "I must have imagined it. I was remembering what you said about that little girl on the ferry, and mermaids. And then I started thinking about how they aren't all nice like in the movies. They used to lure sailors to their death. You know, sirens were a lot like vampires, in a way."

The little girl on the ferry had been frightened by something in the water, Caitlyn remembered, but she didn't mention it to Laurel. She didn't know what it meant, if anything. And she really didn't want to think about sirens or vampires or anything creepy at all. Instead, she bought wristbands for the beachside amusement park.

"The swings were always my favorite when my parents took me to our county fair," Caitlyn said as they waited in line. Even as an adult, she could not deny the thrill of soaring above the ground with her feet dangling and the wind blowing her hair back from her face as the sun began to set.

When the ride ended, Laurel turned to Caitlyn with a big smile. "I wanna go again."

"I've created a monster, haven't I?"

They headed to the roller coaster next, but Laurel was less thrilled. "It's like a minute of complete terror, and then it's over."

"Not unlike my first time," Caitlyn said. She couldn't decide if Laurel looked amused or horrified. "I'm kidding. He was very sweet, and we laughed more than anything, but it was fun." She gazed into the distance. "You know, they never talk about some of the sounds bodies make against other bodies."

Laurel burst out laughing. "Right?"

Caitlyn reached into her bag of cotton candy.

"That guy over there has been watching us," Laurel said in a low voice when her giggling subsided.

"Yeah, they do that," Caitlyn said around a mouthful of sugar. "Annoying."

"No, not like that." Laurel nudged Caitlyn with her shoulder. "Look."

Caitlyn glanced in the direction Laurel indicated. Then she saw him: a familiar-looking man with a buzz cut in a black suit and sunglasses despite the darkening sky. She couldn't tell if he'd caught her looking or not, but he disappeared into a crowd, walking the other direction.

"What was that all about?"

Caitlyn shrugged.

"No idea."

nineteen

. . .

"So, you think he's with the FBI?"

Caitlyn sat on the couch, Max across from her in the chair. He shrugged. "Maybe. He might have been investigating when he helped the biker stop that bartender from dragging you away. What almost happened to you could be related to what happened to Anne Marie, or the bartender could have been another random creep trolling for women at the club."

Caitlyn frowned. "I hope Agent Buzzcut wasn't busy with my stupid ass when he could have been saving her instead."

"You didn't do anything wrong," Max said.

"So, what are Laurel's parents like, anyway?"

Tyler sat beside Caitlyn on the couch with a plate of food. Max rolled his eyes, but if Caitlyn minded the abrupt subject change, she didn't show it. "I dunno, parent-like, I guess. Their house is very… beige. Laurel has the coolest room, though. She isn't like her parents at all."

"Child-like?" Max asked with a straight face.

Now Caitlyn rolled her eyes. "You know what I mean."

"Rarely, if ever," Max said.

Tyler offered Caitlyn a cookie. "Do you know what you're working on this week?"

Caitlyn pointed at her mouth. "We're blocking the seduction scene with Jonathon in Dracula's castle," she said when she was finished chewing. "Mostly a lot of dancing. But I think the intimacy coach is coming in at the end of the week, just to make sure everyone is comfortable with, I dunno, the bed stuff, I guess."

"Fun," Tyler said, looking pained.

Jordan King grumbled. "Where the hell is Billy?"

Max looked at her. "He hasn't come in yet? The rest of the crew has been trickling in."

The stage manager adjusted her headset over her dark brown braids. "He came in when I did, grumbling about throwing his back out moving. I asked him to switch out a couple of gels, but I haven't seen him since. Probably snuck off for a nap." She looked up in the direction of the catwalk. "Billy, you better not be sleeping up there!"

A rooster crowed.

"Hilarious, Tyler." Jordan said into her headset, rolling her eyes at the control booth. She turned back to Max. "Can you unlock the door to the stairwell for the stage crew and costume department? Elliot needs me to wrangle the actors while he meets with the set designer."

Max caught the keys when Jordan tossed them. "It's literally steps from the dressing rooms," he muttered, "but whatever." At least she wasn't asking him to find anything. The basement where they stored props and built sets was sawdust city, and the space above the dressing rooms where they stored costumes reeked of mothballs. His nose itched just thinking about it.

A couple of women with the costume department were waiting by the door. "Susan started measuring the actresses, but she wants us to see what corsets and dresses we can find upstairs," said one.

"Good luck with all that." Max unlocked the door. He flicked on the light in the stairwell, but nothing happened. "Fantastic. I'll be right back."

The women were gone when Max returned with the bulb and a

step stool. He set down the stool and climbed on, trying to ignore how close he was to the stairs leading down to the basement. It always threw off his equilibrium to use stools or stepladders near stairs. The world went topsy-turvy as he struggled against the pull of some imaginary gravitational force that defied physics.

Movement above his head startled him, and he almost lost his balance for real. "What the hell was that?"

"Sorry!" called a voice from upstairs.

"The lights upstairs work, so we just started looking," said another.

Max finished replacing the light bulb. Then he forced himself to go downstairs to check the lights in the basement. When some unseen creature skittered behind some cans of paint, he didn't worry. Not at first.

"Just a rat," Max told himself.

So why could he hear it breathing from across the room, even over the pounding of his own heartbeat?

Claws scraped against the floor as something pulled its way out from behind the paint. Max didn't wait to see what it was. He ran back up the stairs, slamming the door shut. Let the stage crew handle it. His job duties did not include pest control.

"Sarah—that's the intimacy coach—she's here today. So we're blocking the beginning of the scene first, then working on the dances for the rest of the week," Amelia explained to Caitlyn while the costume designer measured her for her corset.

"Try to hold still this time so I can get an accurate measurement," Susan said, wrapping a tape measure around Caitlyn's waist.

"Sorry." Caitlyn giggled. "I'm ticklish."

"It's a good thing we're doing most of the touching in this scene," Emma said. "You'd never make it through otherwise. How are you ever going to play a romantic lead if someone can't even touch your side without you losing it?"

"It's not all the time." Caitlyn was indignant. "Just when I know that I shouldn't laugh. And the more I think about how I shouldn't laugh, the harder it gets not to laugh."

Amelia and Emma raised their eyebrows.

"Okay, yeah, I get how being on stage in front of an audience is one of those times you're not supposed to laugh," Caitlyn said, "but as long as I'm in character, I'm fine. I swear." She crossed her fingers behind her back. "Unless the character would also laugh, I suppose."

"Well, you managed to hold it together this time," Susan said as she turned to write on a legal pad.

"Isn't this exciting?" Emma said. "I overheard Elliot talking to some of the crew and he wants to start having dress rehearsals as soon as the costumes are ready. If everything goes smoothly, we'll start performing for an audience in just a few weeks."

"That's a big 'if'," Amelia said. "Right now, I'm just grateful to have a steady paycheck and my evenings free to visit my grandmother. That all changes once we go live."

"How is your grandmother?" Caitlyn asked.

"She seems to be settling into the residential facility well enough, and she likes her roommate," Amelia said, "but the food is awful, so she likes it when I bring dinner. I'm supposed to smuggle in some salt and pepper tonight."

Jordan poked her head into the dressing room. "Elliot and Sarah are ready for you on stage now," she said.

"Still no sign of Billy?" Tyler asked.

Max shook his head. "I was gonna check the catwalk, but Jordan asked me to help you with the bed. Maybe he's doing some other odd job."

"A little further right," Elliot barked from the audience. "I need it off-center."

Tyler and Max pushed the bed over.

"Now angle it toward the center. It's too straight." Elliot looked away from Max and Tyler to continue talking to the set designer, Dave. The middle-aged man scribbled notes as Elliot talked and gestured at the stage.

"When's the rest of the crew coming in?"

"This week," Max said, grunting as they repositioned the heavy wooden bed. "Some already started trickling in today. And Jordan said she's gonna see about getting her little brother a job."

"Amari? Isn't he, like, seventeen?" Tyler wiped a bead of sweat from his brow.

"And a varsity linebacker," Max said. "He'll be fine. Annoying, no doubt, but fine." He followed Tyler offstage. "Anyway, it's good to have experience in all aspects of the theater if we ever want to move on to bigger and better things. You don't want to work the soundboard forever, do you?"

"Do you really think you could do his job?" Tyler tilted his head in Elliot's direction as they walked to the control booth.

"Billy could do his job," Max said. "And he'd be a lot nicer about it, too. Dude had Maya in tears last week when you were looking for the extra microphones. Andre had to talk her down from quitting, and things got pretty heated between Sarah and Elliot, too. Does Maya strike you as someone who cries easily?"

Tyler shook his head. "It must have been really bad."

The intimacy coordinator's trust exercises had everyone laughing before they walked to the large wooden bed near center stage. Sarah was in her thirties, with dark hair pulled back into a bun and a broad smile. "Okay, so as a reminder before we start choreographing this scene, Michael's boundaries begin and end here." The woman gestured at her lower belly and upper thighs.

Michael nodded. "Everything else is fair game. Just don't bite too hard."

"Stage bites only," Sarah said. "I don't know if everyone's had their shots." The group laughed. "Ladies, I know you've said you feel comfortable with each other, but, just like Michael, it's okay to pause the scene if something doesn't feel right or you need to adjust your personal boundaries." She turned to the audience. "Elliot, do you have anything to add?" The way she asked made it sound like she hoped the answer was 'no.'

"Let's see what they come up with first," he said, matching Sarah's even tone.

Sarah nodded. She turned to the group with an encouraging smile.

Caitlyn felt something drop on the back of her neck. She wiped it away without a second thought as she crawled on top of the bed and ran her hand up Michael's thigh. He sat up as Amelia approached from the other side and Emma crawled beside him to caress his face. Caitlyn felt another drop. This time she looked at her hand. There was a streak of red. She watched as Amelia brushed something from her cheek, then looked down as more drops fell, hitting the bed and staining the white sheets. They looked down then stared at each other. Caitlyn saw her fear and confusion mirrored on Amelia's face.

"What the hell?"

"That's not in the script, Michael," Elliot snapped.

Emma looked up at the catwalk. She screamed, clutching Michael's arm in terror.

twenty

. . .

"He was so excited about having his own place again." Jordan brushed a tear from her cheek. She leaned against Max, sniffling. "Are the police still here?"

Max handed her a tissue. He sat beside her in the control room, an arm around her shoulder. "I think they're still interviewing some of the actors."

"I don't know why the police came instead of like, animal control or something." Tyler leaned against the back wall. "A person couldn't have done that. His throat was torn all to hell." Jordan released a loud sob. Max turned, sending Tyler a look of death.

"I bet it's whatever's been gnawing on all the cables," Tyler continued, oblivious. "Probably one of those rabid raccoons we've been hearing about. They got tired of mangling each other. Now they've moved on to people."

"A raccoon?" Now Jordan turned to glare at Tyler, dark eyes flashing. "Honestly!"

"I've been telling people. They can be really aggressive," Tyler said. "I heard Nick say one chased him the other night when he was taking his dog for a walk. At least he thought it was a raccoon. Couldn't get a clear look at it—on account of the running away, the coward. It was one of those yippy ankle biters, too."

"The raccoon?"

"No, his dog. Nick has a corgi. For the ladies, obviously." Tyler rolled his eyes.

"That tracks." Jordan sniffled, but she was no longer crying.

Max watched as a few police officers still milled around the stage, one talking to Elliot. "I'm not inclined to superstition," he said, "but sometimes this whole production really does feel like it's cursed."

"There's no such thing as curses, Em." Amelia rolled her eyes as she followed Emma into the dressing room.

Caitlyn walked in behind them and shut the door before sinking into a chair. She felt ill.

"Did *you* do it?"

"Do what?" Sophia turned and stared at Emma. "Tear some poor guy's throat out?"

"She thinks someone said the 'm' word in the theater or something, and that's why things keep going wrong," Amelia said. "You should have seen the look on the cop's face when she told him he should ask everyone if they mentioned The Scottish Play."

"That's hardly the craziest thing the police have seen or heard today," Maya said, without a trace of amusement in her voice. "Lloyd gave *his* interview in character. And get this. Johan's threatening to quit. His first official day of rehearsal, and someone dies. Between Anne Marie's vanishing act, and now this, things don't look great whether you believe in curses or not."

"I did not land this gig just to lose it again," the new cast member, Hailey, said. "I feel bad about whatever happened to that techie, I do, but it had to be a freak accident. When's the last time you heard about a wild animal attack in a theater?"

Caitlyn swayed as she stood up. Her stomach turned.

"Where are you going?" Laurel asked.

"I just need some air."

. . .

As Caitlyn wobbled down the hallway, she heard Leanne's voice.

"I was in my dressing room all morning," Leanne was saying, talking to a couple of police officers in the hallway. She stood with her door open just a crack. Caitlyn met her eyes when she said, "I didn't see or hear anything."

Were her cheeks looking rosier than usual?

Caitlyn looked away. She continued down the hall and walked outside to the alley. To her surprise, she found Nicholas sitting with his hands on his knees, staring at nothing in particular. He turned to give her a wan smile.

"I dunno why I'm so weirded out," he said. "I didn't even see the body. Michael seems pretty chill about the whole thing. Emma's talons did a number on his arm, though. How are you?" He patted the pavement next to him. The concern crossing his face appeared genuine.

"Better than Billy," Caitlyn said, sitting beside him. "Sorry. I'm a terrible person."

"Nah." Nicholas rested a hand on her shoulder. "We all handle grief in our own ways."

"I never actually met hi—"Caitlyn started to say.

"It's like me and Anne Marie," Nicholas continued. "We never, like, made it official. The breakup, I mean. Now she's gone, and I never even got a chance to say I'm sorry." He looked down, morose.

A little too busy boning her best friend, Caitlyn thought, then felt guilty. "I understand," she said. "I almost never have any closure." It was true. Most of her relationships just sort of fizzled without anybody saying anything. Nobody had flat-out disappeared, though.

"It's nice having someone who gets it." Nicholas gave her shoulder a gentle squeeze.

Caitlyn looked down at his hand on her shoulder, then at him. "Nick?"

"Yes?" His green eyes gazed into hers.

"I'm going back inside now. You can let go."

"Oh, right. Sorry."

Nick released Caitlyn's shoulder. Then he gave her what she

supposed was his approximation of an apologetic grin, but he looked about as contrite as a fox with a mouthful of chicken feathers.

Tyler walked into the office where Manny Ortega sat behind the desk, clutching a baseball cap against his chest. He was an older man with graying hair, a growing bald spot, and a congenial smile—except for this particular instance.

"You okay?" Tyler asked him.

"Billy was one of my first hires when I took over this place." Manny gazed out the window even though there was nothing to see but the back alley. "He wasn't skilled at anything in particular, but man, did he love the theater. You could ask him to help out anywhere, and he'd do it, no complaints."

Alas, poor Billy, we hardly knew ye, Tyler thought with a twinge of guilt. He wondered why Billy hadn't asked anyone for help before going up to the catwalk. *I probably would have made up an excuse even if he had,* Tyler realized. That made him feel even worse.

"The police are wrapping things up," he told Manny. "They searched the entire building but only found a couple rats. Whatever attacked Billy was…bigger." His frown deepened. "Elliot's sending the cast home for the day, but he wants everyone back tomorrow morning as scheduled."

"Yeah, I told him I thought rehearsals should be put on hiatus for the rest of the week out of respect, and for the obvious safety concerns. I wasn't gonna charge him rent or nothing, but he insisted." Manny turned to Tyler, frowning. "I guess there's a lot of pressure on him to get this production in front of an audience in a few weeks."

"A few weeks? Really?"

"The show must go on," Manny said with a bleak smile that didn't reach his eyes.

"The Scottish Play? Really?" Max rolled his eyes. "I suppose Leanne could be Lady Macbeth, persuading Elliot to slaughter classic literature and musical theater in one fell swoop." He sat down on the couch.

"She definitely has blood on her hands for that wretched duet with Michael. But I'd never be dumb enough to say so out loud in the theater. I don't really think Billy's death had anything to do with any silly superstitions, though."

"But you think Leanne has something to do with it." Caitlyn sat beside him.

"I was being facetious," Max said, turning to her.

"But what if you're onto something," Caitlyn pressed. "Think about it. First Anne Marie was spending all this time with Leanne. And I don't know if you ever noticed, but the more time they spent together, the paler and sicklier Anne Marie started to look. And then there was the time I saw them at the club, just before she disappeared. And now Billy is dead."

"Billy was attacked by a wild animal."

"But what if he wasn't? How did a wild animal even get into the theater?" Max looked skeptical, but Caitlyn hurried on before Max could argue. "What if the reason Leanne has become a sort of muse for Elliot is because she really is a…"

"Please don't say it."

"Vampire."

Max took Caitlyn's hands in his own. "You've been through a lot these past few weeks. Between losing your apartment and all the stress and chaos of the theater even before you factor in deaths and disappearances, it makes sense that you'd feel…overwhelmed. Maybe you should consider talking to someone."

Caitlyn pulled her hands away. "I'm not crazy."

"Neither am I," Max said, "but I still have someone I talk to, and not just because of the big life changes. Everyone can benefit from an outside perspective now and then."

"Yeah, well, I'll try to squeeze it into my schedule." Caitlyn looked up as the door opened. Tyler walked in with a bag full of takeout. She rose from the couch to help him empty the contents.

"They were out of fortune cookies; can you believe it? Supply chain issues or something, I dunno." Tyler shrugged.

"That feels ominous," Max said. "If a little too on the nose."

twenty-one

. . .

"Caitlyn was quiet this morning." Tyler sat in the chair beside Max in the control booth. He looked out at the stage where Andre appeared to be trying to coax a smile out of Caitlyn. "Guess they're working on other stuff until Sarah can come back to finish blocking the scene with Michael."

"She's probably still upset about Billy," Max said. "Caitlyn, I mean."

"Obviously," Tyler said. "But at least she said 'good morning' to me. She didn't say anything to you at all."

On stage, Andre's efforts appeared to be successful. Caitlyn laughed as he pulled her in close, then spun her away. Then Caitlyn turned to Amelia when Emma cut in. Andre loved the attention, no doubt.

Max sighed. "Caitlyn thinks Leanne is a vampire and that she killed Anne Marie and Billy. I said she should consider talking to someone, you know, a professional? She didn't seem to appreciate the suggestion."

"Andre, maybe," Tyler mused.

"I don't think he's a licensed therapist, though she certainly enjoys his company."

"No, maybe he's the vampire. Talk about typecasting."

"It's obviously not Andre," Max said with a withering glare. "It's obviously not anyone because vampires don't exist," he amended.

"Maybe it's you," Tyler said.

"I'm not a vampire."

"That's exactly what a vampire would say."

"And people think I'm abnormal." Max rolled his eyes.

"You wanna see something weird?"

Amelia reached into the loose-fitting top she wore over a sports bra and pulled out a cross on a beaded chain to show Caitlyn.

"Not weird," Caitlyn said. "Ironic, maybe?"

"It's been sitting in my jewelry box for years," Amelia said, "but last night when I went to visit my grandmother, she was upset. Someone at the center had died the night before. Not all that surprising under normal circumstances, but he was new and not very sick. Just needed more care than his family could provide at home. Like my grandmother. Anyway, this terrifying howl woke her up at, like, three in the morning. She was certain she dreamt it. The next day, she found out the new resident had died. None of the staff would say anything specific, but she overheard a couple of nurses talking. They said he died of fright. Between her story, and what happened here, I guess I'm feeling sort of on edge. It's all so creepy."

"Understandable." Caitlyn felt a chill run through her veins. She decided not to share her theory with Amelia. The actress was scared enough as it was. After the way Max reacted last night, she thought it best not to tell anyone, not even Laurel.

"Ladies."

Johan took a deep bow in front of them before walking on stage to rehearse. *Guess he decided to stick around after all.*

"He is *fine*." Hailey's gaze came to rest on the backside of a tall muscular stagehand as he carried lumber down the hallway. She wiped her hands with a napkin and threw it in the trash can beside the dressing room door.

"He's my brother," Jordan said, following her into the dressing room. "He's a junior."

"NYU?"

"High school."

Hailey grimaced. "Don't suppose you have any older brothers?"

"Sorry, no. Isabella needs everyone in the ballroom scene on stage so we can get Hailey up to speed." Jordan looked down at her clipboard. "Dracula's brides, Elliot wants to hear how your songs are coming along in the green room."

"Caitlyn, you're looking a little strained on some of the higher notes," Elliot said after she finished singing "The Children of the Night" with Andre, Amelia, and Emma. She bit her bottom lip, ears burning.

"I think her voice is opening up beautifully." A trace of annoyance flicked across Diane's face. "You sound wonderful," she assured Caitlyn.

Amelia reached for Caitlyn's hand and gave it a gentle squeeze.

"I agree," Andre said. "The way these ladies harmonize, it more than makes up for the song's...lyrical shortcomings."

"James Merrick is a respected lyricist and composer." Elliot's cool gaze shifted away from Caitlyn and came to rest on Andre's face.

"He rhymed night with fright," Andre folded his arms across his chest. "It's insipid."

Elliot's jaw tightened.

"It's a shame the other gentlemen are busy dancing," Diane said, "because the final confrontation is coming together nicely. Very dramatic and powerful. Perhaps Johan and Andre could show you their duet while the ladies rest their voices? We only started working on it yesterday before all the...unpleasantness, but they're such wonderful foils for each other."

Elliot turned to Diane. "I'd like to see it. And maybe Andre's earlier scene with Lloyd, too. Just to ensure that everyone has good chemistry." His eyes returned to Andre, who stared back, unimpressed. "Ladies, go run your lines or do whatever it is you do to amuse yourselves in the dressing room."

"The producers would replace Elliot's creepy butt before they ever replaced Andre," Emma said when they walked into the dressing room. "And what does he think we do in here? Have pillow fights? He wishes!"

"Mostly we just talk trash," Amelia said. "I doubt the guys are any better."

"I think I have more to worry about than Andre does." Caitlyn sat and stared at her morose reflection in the mirror.

"Elliot's just messing with you," Amelia said, patting her back. "Don't let him get into your head. You should hear some of the horror stories Maya has told me. Even Leanne hasn't been spared his wrath, and she's practically his muse. The only one burning any bridges is Elliot."

"I know we haven't been the nicest to Leanne," Emma said, "but I feel kind of bad. I doubt he treats her any better in private. Probably why she's always so quiet and mopey. Maybe I should invite her to hang out after rehearsal some time. With Anne Marie gone and Maya keeping her distance, she could probably use a friend."

Caitlyn turned to her. "Are you sure that's a good idea? Maybe Maya is right to keep her distance."

"I love Maya," Amelia said, "don't get me wrong, but she got a taste of stardom on the road, and now she has no time for anyone or anything else. I think the only reason she's fine with playing Lucy instead of Mina is because it's the flashier role."

"I'm gonna see if Leanne is in her dressing room. Isabella usually gives everyone a break around now."

Caitlyn's frown deepened as she watched Emma go.

"Oh, don't look so worried. It's only Leanne. It's not like she's going to bite Emma's head off. That's Elliot's deal. Though I find myself regretting my choice of words after yesterday." She reached for her cross through her shirt and twiddled it absently.

"So that was weird." Emma walked back into the dressing room and sat across from Caitlyn and Amelia.

"She wasn't there?" Amelia asked.

"No, she's there, but she did not want me to come in." Emma shook her head. "I think she's afraid of Elliot. Said he wouldn't like it."

"Maybe Anne Marie was getting too close," Amelia said. "Maybe he gets jealous."

"A crazy jealous boyfriend," Emma mused. "What could possibly go wrong?"

"Catie, how long are you gonna keep giving Max the silent treatment?"

"What?" Caitlyn looked up from her bowl of ramen. Max and Tyler sat across from her chair on the couch with their own bowls. "No, I'm not...it's not that." She proceeded to tell them about the exchange with Elliot and Emma's brief encounter with Leanne. "I'm guessing a vampire wouldn't be afraid of a mere mortal," she finished.

"To be fair, I've never seen Leanne *or* Elliot outside during the day," Tyler said. "I think they're always the last to leave."

"How is that helpful?" Max glared at Tyler. He started to say something else, then appeared to reconsider. "Then again, it does suggest that Leanne and Elliot might have had something to do with Anne Marie's disappearance after all. Like, maybe you really did see them all at the club, and there was a confrontation, and either she left them or they left her, and that's when someone took her."

"And now they feel guilty because it's their fault," Tyler said. "That could certainly add to the strain on their relationship. And he's now taking it out on others, and that's really not cool."

"I think he's just an asshole in general," Max said, "but no, definitely not cool."

"Still doesn't explain what happened to Billy," Caitlyn said.

"No." Max frowned. "Just a weird freaky coincidence. That's all."

Separate, unrelated threats. Caitlyn did not find that possibility reassuring.

twenty-two

. . .

"How is everyone? Really?" Sarah's gaze traveled to each of the bed scene's players as they waited in the hall. "I asked Elliot if he considered bringing in a grief counselor after what happened, but he didn't feel it was necessary."

Caitlyn shrugged. "It was seriously scary, but we never even met him. I don't wanna, like, hijack the crew's grief, you know?" She found herself wondering if she ever asked Max and Tyler how they were, but she had been too wrapped up in her own nonsense to consider their feelings about what happened.

"Okay, I just want to remind everyone this is a safe space to talk if anyone has anything they want to say before we block this scene," Sarah said.

"This is a pretty solid group," Michael said. "Everyone has everyone's back, I think."

Most everyone, anyway, Caitlyn thought.

Tyler's brow furrowed as he watched Caitlyn crawl onto the bed on stage.

"I don't think any more dead bodies will be hanging from the catwalk today if that's what you're worried about," Max said. "Everyone's present and accounted for. Even Jordan's little brother, who isn't completely annoying for a high school jock, after all… and not exactly little."

"The jocks always turned out for the spring musical at my school, the ones that didn't play baseball anyway," Tyler said. "Usually to perform, though."

"Same," said Max. "They weren't so bad. I guess I'm getting grumpy in my old age."

"Yeah, as a wizened twenty-two-year-old crank you may as well have one foot in the grave." Tyler looked back at the stage, where Caitlyn, Amelia, and Emma appeared to be getting even cozier with each other than with Michael. "Now there's a guy who's died and gone to heaven. Meanwhile, I'm in literal hell."

Max patted Tyler on the back. "You'll live."

"You're kidding me, right?"

Offstage, Jordan stared at the stunt coordinator in horror. Johnny Bianchi gazed at her with a mild expression as he folded his arms across his muscular chest. "Steve already has experience with aerial work, so he's agreed to be the sailor who gets pulled up to the catwalk."

"The catwalk? Have you heard about the stuff happening around here?"

"Yeah, I know about the lights, but I checked the rigging. It's fine."

"What about that… animal that killed Billy? That had nothing to do with rigging."

"Do you really think that's likely to happen again?" Johnny softened his tone. "Manny and Elliot told me that they instituted a buddy system. There will always be at least two people on the catwalk, which we usually do for aerial stunt work anyway. We aren't working on that until next week, when Elliot expects the boat to be ready. He promised me the stage for a full afternoon before he starts running the first act in its entirety—"

Jordan started to speak, but the stunt coordinator continued. "—

which is plenty of time to lock down the choreography. We're starting to block the fight scenes in the second act this week. Did Luis find the prop swords? We need them after lunch."

"I didn't see any on his prop table." Jordan sighed, defeated. "I'll send Luis or Amari downstairs to get them, whoever I see first."

"Wish we got swords," Amelia said to Caitlyn as they stood back and watched the men work through some basic fencing techniques with the stunt coordinator. "All we get to do is lunge and hiss lyrics at them —like that'll do anything—and then die."

The men already wore bits and pieces of their costumes. Andre in particular needed to practice fighting in his wig and flowing velvet robes. Christopher was a natural as he blocked and evaded Johnny's attacks. Nicholas was competent if sweaty and out of breath; Matthew, suitably overwhelmed. "This looks so much easier in *Diablo*," he joked.

"And Elliot expects us to fight and sing at the same time?" Nicholas wiped sweat from his brow. "Never thought I'd say this, but I'm worried I might not have the stamina."

"And I'm all out of potions," Matthew attempted to quip.

"Huh?"

"Gatorade," Matthew clarified.

"Oh. Right."

The most elaborate fight sequence was between Michael and Andre. Though Michael was slighter than Andre, his deft moves gave him the appearance of a formidable opponent. Caitlyn leaned back on her elbows to watch from the side, where she'd "died," as the actors moved across the stage. It really was a dance, as elegant as anything Isabella had choreographed. It ended with Andre standing victorious over Michael. Then Johan leapt in front of Michael, holding out his cross, but the big finish was left to Leanne as Andre cowered.

"Of course *she* gets a sword," Caitlyn heard Emma mutter.

Leanne turned to Johnny with a look of uncertainty as she stood behind Andre, blade raised over her head.

"We'll stop right there for now," he said, grinning.

Leanne lowered the sword. Caitlyn realized she had been holding her breath as if there had been something to worry about. The rehearsal began with Johnny demonstrating that all the swords had blunt retractable tips and no sharp edges. "At worst, you might get a little sore and bruised if someone hits you hard enough," he'd assured them.

"There are a lot of moving pieces in this show, so some of the blocking might change in the next couple of weeks." Johnny looked to Elliot in the audience for confirmation. Elliot nodded. "The plan is that Dracula will cower behind a pillar or a statue or something," Johnny continued, "and while the audience will see Jonathon swing the sword, they won't see Dracula lose his head. Instead, Van Helsing will reach behind the pillar to retrieve a prop head."

"I wanted to stick to practical effects as much as possible," Andre said, "but Elliot insists that his production have a run of more than one night."

Everyone laughed. Everyone but Elliot, who was on his feet, approaching the side of the stage. "What can I say?" He climbed the stairs and walked to Andre. "I'm not willing to sacrifice my star performer." Elliot held out his hand. "Excellent work today."

Andre shook his hand. "I'm only as good as my fellow actors." He bowed, his eyes coming to rest on Caitlyn. He winked, straightened, and removed his wig.

"What was that all about it?"

Caitlyn turned to look at Jordan. "What was what all about?"

"I saw the way Andre looked at you," Jordan said. "There's not something going on between you two, is there?"

"You mean the wink?" Caitlyn laughed. "Nah, it's not like that. Probably has to do with a disagreement between Andre and Elliot yesterday." She continued walking into the hallway.

"I don't wanna be hearing about any fights between those two," Jordan said, following. "Thirsty performers are bad enough. A clash of the Titans is a whole other…" Jordan trailed off as she saw her brother in the hall, perfectly still as he faced away from them. "Amari?

He didn't respond.

"Amari?" Jordan repeated. "Amari, what's wrong?"

Jordan's brother turned to her with haunted eyes as he said, "I saw a rat downstairs."

"It's New York City, baby. We see lots of rats."

Amari's expression froze. "This one didn't have a head."

twenty-three

. . .

"I'm sorry, but after what happened to that poor techie, I'm finding it a little hard to get broken up about a dead rat," Jennifer said the next morning.

"Amari's probably one of those gentle giant types," Cassidy said. "He must have been so upset."

"How do we know that rat wasn't killed by whatever killed Billy?"

"Don't be stupid," Elise said to Sophia. "Whatever killed Billy would have done more than just bite off its head. Someone probably left a door or a window open a crack, and a stray cat got inside the building."

"Everyone's talking about what Amari saw, but no one is talking about what he didn't."

Everyone turned to look at Laurel in surprise.

"What's that?" Amelia's voice was kind.

"More rats," Laurel said.

"So…?" Elise asked.

"She's got a point," Emma said. "When's the last time you saw just one rat in a building? Especially this one. I used to hear them all the time. Now I can't remember the last time I heard one."

"Well, something's been running around the building," Caitlyn said. "Must be whatever killed the rat."

"Oh my God, can we please stop talking about dead things?" Hailey shuddered.

Emma rolled her eyes. "Yeah, let's go rehearse our musical. About dead things."

"Honestly, I wouldn't be surprised if Lloyd mistook that rat for one of his gummies," Emma said. She glanced over her shoulder at the green room, where some of the men were running lines.

"I heard he's moved on from worms to snakes and tarantulas," Amelia said.

Caitlyn nodded. "Laurel said he stuck one down the back of Matt's shirt the other day. Matt played it off. He has older brothers, so it takes a lot to rattle him." She tilted her head, considering. "Shame it wasn't Nick."

"Omigod, I'd pay him to do it to Nick."

"I doubt he takes requests," Amelia told Emma. After a beat: "Elliot would be better."

"Omigod, yes!"

"Omigod, shut up," Jordan said, poking her head into the hallway. "They can hear you on stage." She turned off her headset. "But I can chip in a few bucks if Lloyd's willing to take Elliot's pasty ass down a peg or two. That boy's a menace."

The women dissolved into giggles as Jordan pressed a finger to her lips.

Tyler looked at Max in concern. His roommate sat hunched over his chair, arms wrapped around himself, skin pale.

"You feelin' okay?"

"Haven't felt right since lunch," Max said.

"I bet it was the salad. That's why I don't eat my veggies. You ever hear about French fries getting recalled for *e. coli*? No! It's always the greens." He looked away from Max to watch as the performers practiced the final fight scene on the stage below. Tyler couldn't tell if Caitlyn was sleeping or just bored as she sprawled out in faux death.

Max groaned. "I'll be right back." He bolted from the control room.

"Have fun storming the restroom!" Tyler called after him.

Down below, things were looking a little strange. Nicholas appeared sweatier than usual as he wiped his brow. Even Christopher was running out of steam. Then Emma leapt up from the floor and ran off stage. "Oh yeah," Tyler said, leaning back in his chair, "definitely the salad."

"This is why I bring my own lunch," Jordan said to her brother. They stood offstage as Elliot glared down at his clipboard.

The director had ended rehearsal a couple hours early for the cast, but most of the crew remained to work on building and painting set pieces. Not everyone who had the catered lunch was ill, but losing a third of the cast was enough to throw a wrench in the rest of the day's plans. "The good news is it's probably nothing serious like *e. coli* or salmonella," Elliot said. "But we can probably expect limited attendance tomorrow. I'll figure out what we can work on in the morning."

Jordan nodded.

"No matter what, we need to start running Act One next week. The producers are anxious to get this production in front of an audience so we can make any changes as needed for a real Broadway run. I don't care if we have to keep vomit bags off stage, we're adhering to the schedule. Maybe we'll do away with the extravagance of a catered lunch. Save some money."

Jordan sighed as she watched the director stalk off. She hoped his ambitions wouldn't be the death of them. Then she remembered the events of the past week and shuddered.

"Things always this exciting in the theater?" asked Amari.

"It's only been a week, and already I long for the tedium of opening and closing curtains in between shushing silly actors," Jordan said, linking arms with her brother. "Let's get out of here before anything else goes wrong."

. . .

"I hope Elliot doesn't expect me to do much more than turn the lights on and off," Tyler said Friday morning on the way to the theater. They'd left Max to sleep off his illness at home. "I still gotta find one of the sound effects tapes—the Halloween one—unless Nick's corgi has a convincing howl."

"I feel bad leaving Max home alone," Caitlyn said. "Jen's okay, but she stayed home to take care of Cass. Maybe one of us should have stayed with Max."

"Nah, he'll probably enjoy having the place to himself." Tyler grimaced as he opened the back door. "Well, as much as anyone can enjoy anything with food poisoning. He likes his privacy anyway."

"I hope he knows how much I appreciate you guys letting me stay with you. Jen and Cass expect their roommate to reach a decision soon," Caitlyn said, walking past him. "I know you must be sick of my hair clogging up the sink."

"I'll miss waking up to you in the morning." The words were out of his mouth before Tyler could consider how they'd sound out loud. His cheeks reddened. "Oh, look, it's Lloyd. Hey Lloyd, how ya doin' bud?"

The actor held a finger to his lips as he scurried down the hallway.

"What a weird dude." Tyler watched him go, shaking his head.

Caitlyn's brow furrowed. "Was he coming out of Maya's dressing room?"

"Leanne's fine, pale, maybe, but that's nothing new. Does she even eat?"

Caitlyn figured Amelia's question was rhetorical, but she hadn't ruled out vampirism.

"I haven't seen Maya yet, but I know she's fine. Emma, not so much," Amelia continued, her expression twisting with worry. "Do you know about Elise?"

Sophia shrugged. "The question is 'do I care'?" She looked around the dressing room, catching the women's eyes in the mirrors. "The answer is 'no'. No, I do not."

"Noted," Amelia arched an eyebrow as she studied Sophia for a moment before turning back to the other women. "That leaves us short one vampire bride and half the women in the chorus."

"Matt's coming," Laurel spoke up, "but Chris isn't. Nick looked pretty bad when we—"

She was interrupted by a shrill scream.

Caitlyn followed Amelia into the hall. They ran to Maya's dressing room.

"Maya? Maya, open up!"

twenty-four

. . .

Amelia banged on the door. When Maya didn't answer, she tried the doorknob. It opened. Maya huddled in the corner of her dressing room, eyes wide and staring. Amelia crouched down in front of her.

"I was just talking to Andre yesterday," Maya said. "He was so full of life."

Caitlyn looked in the room. She gasped.

Someone's head—just their head—was face down on the vanity counter in a puddle of blood, surrounded by a mass of hair the same color as Andre's Dracula wig. Caitlyn backed out of the room in shock. She leaned against the wall in the hallway and slid down until her rear touched the dingy carpeted floor.

"Tell Luis to keep looking! I can't put out more than one fire at a time," Jordan muttered into her headset as she walked past Caitlyn into Maya's dressing room. "Huh. Maybe I *can* put out more than one fire at a time. Found it!" The other women watched in horror as Jordan lifted the head off the counter. "Oh, what the—" Jordan put the head back down. She lifted a blood-stained hand to her nose and sniffed. "Corn syrup. That creepy little man put stage blood all over the head. Lloyd did this, I know it."

"It's…it's not real?"

Amelia helped Maya to her feet. She stared at Jordan in disbelief.

"This look like Andre to you?"

Jordan picked the head back up, holding the face in Maya's direction.

"I can't believe anyone would play a mean trick like that," Amelia said. She helped Maya to her feet.

"Tyler and I did see Lloyd sneaking around the hallway when we came in this morning." Caitlyn stood up; her cheeks flushed in anger. "I even thought he was leaving Maya's room. I'm sorry, Maya. I should have checked first."

Maya gave her a wan smile. "It's not your fault, Cate." Her face darkened. "I swear, when I see Lloyd, I'm going to wring his scrawny neck."

"Get in line," Jordan said.

Caitlyn noticed Leanne standing with her door open a crack. She looked guilty and even a little sad. When Leanne saw Caitlyn, she lowered her eyes and pushed the door shut. She must have heard Lloyd and that maniacal giggle of his while he was leaving his "present" for Maya. Caitlyn still couldn't believe it. Dropping gummy worms down Matthew's shirt was bad enough. Leaving a head in someone's dressing room crossed an obvious line.

"I heard Elliot laid into him for a full five minutes," Jordan told Caitlyn in a low voice as they watched Lloyd slink offstage. "I guess he's been on the outs with Broadway for a while now, probably because of fool stunts like this. It's a wonder Elliot didn't fire him on the spot. And after what happened to Billy." Jordan shook her head. "Did you know his throat had been torn up so bad, it nearly decapitated him?"

"I do now." Caitlyn grimaced. The actress's already pale skin was even paler.

"Oh, no," Jordan said, patting her back. "I don't need any more actors getting sick. Elliot wants to run through the bedroom scene without Emma later, to get an idea of how it looks and sounds with fog effects and lighting. Tyler's been giving Amari a crash course on running the light board." She sighed. "Guess I should go track down the dry ice. Luis is still trying to find a new wig for the head. There's corn syrup all over it, and the last thing we want to do is attract any more cockroaches. Lloyd is bad enough."

"Do you want me to come with you downstairs? They don't need me for anything at the moment," Caitlyn said, the color returning to her cheeks. As the stage cleared of performers, stagehands started setting up for the ship scene.

Jordan shook her head. "Nah, there's plenty of crew down there. But thanks." She walked into the hall, heading for the stairs. A couple stagehands walked toward her, carrying a crow's nest and sail. Jordan took a step back into the doorway of the women's dressing room to let them pass. Another walked by with the helm. So many moving pieces. *What a nightmare.* At least Elliot was taking a minimalist approach.

Downstairs, the basement was noisy with the sound of hammers and power tools and people shouting to one another. Jordan wrinkled her nose as she searched rows of paint, tools, and other supplies until she found the dry ice, locating it in a dark corner near the very end of the room. As she hefted a container, Jordan thought she heard something growl. *Just a power sander, dumbass.*

Still, Jordan made a hasty retreat.

"Hey, you need help with that?" a member of the crew asked.

"Nah, I'm good," Jordan grunted as she ascended the stairs, hoping she didn't look as unnerved as she felt.

"What a slow day." Amelia stretched and yawned as she joined Caitlyn backstage.

"Monday will be better," Caitlyn said. "I heard Susan already has a lot of costumes ready for us to try on in between scenes. But after this morning, I kind of appreciate working at a slower pace."

"Tell me about it," Amelia said. "Maya is so pissed. On the bright side, Elliot's playing nice around her. Guess he doesn't want to lose another Lucy. Word is the only reason Lloyd didn't get fired is he still has one high-powered friend left in this town. But I think he'll be keeping a low profile from here on out."

They watched as stagehands placed tape on the stage. Elliot had already approved the positioning of the bed. The stage was otherwise empty apart from a nightstand with some LED candles and a single flat painted to resemble a stone wall behind the bed. It had gargoyle-shaped sconces on either side and a couple more LED candles.

Movement caught Caitlyn's eye. Michael was doing a silly dance to entertain himself on the other side of the stage. She laughed.

"I've got the first batches of dry ice ready to go," Jordan said into her headset.

"Alright, everyone. Let's see how this scene looks with special effects," Caitlyn heard Elliot say in the audience. "Once Jonathon is in position, start the fog, and have the brides crawl onto the stage. Actually, you know what? I want to see how it looks if they crawl up the stairs on either side of the stage. As long as it's dark enough during the scene change, the audience shouldn't notice them getting into position. Then a spotlight on the bed when the curtains open should pull their focus center stage."

Amelia sighed. "I'll take the other side."

Caitlyn walked to the stairs on her side and crouched down.

"Hey, Tyler?" Elliot said into his headset. "Cue the wolf howl. Jordan, let's start with the curtains closed. After the scene change is finished, a wolf will howl. As the curtain opens, fog should already be moving across the stage." To Caitlyn and Amelia, he said, "Then the brides go." He waited for Jordan to close the curtains. "Alright then. Action."

A wolf howled, the curtains opened, and fog rolled across the stage. Caitlyn began to crawl up the stairs and onto the stage. "Try to keep it slow and sexy, ladies. If you can," Elliot called. Caitlyn hoped he couldn't see her lip curl into a sneer as she approached the end of the bed. Practicing without Emma meant more work for Amelia and Caitlyn, so she felt relief when Elliot said, "You know what? That's looking pretty good. I like the backlighting with the reds and violets." He paused. "I think we want to bring down the spotlight once the brides are in motion, though. It's washing them out too much. Vampires or not, they need to look hot, not sickly."

Amelia rolled her eyes at Caitlyn.

"Let's try it again, this time bringing down the spotlight."

After a couple more run-throughs, Elliot seemed satisfied with the scene. "I definitely want you both crawling up the stairs. Again, try to make it sexy. You're vampires, not zombies. When Emma gets back, she can crawl from behind the flat. I think we're good for tonight. Hopefully we have a full cast on Monday. I want to start running the first act in its entirety."

As Elliot left and everyone else cleared the stage, Michael came up to Caitlyn. "Hey, Cate, can I ask you about something?" He ran a hand through his blond hair, looking nervous. And Michael never looked nervous.

A wolf howled. Caitlyn looked up at the control booth, raising an eyebrow. Silence. She turned back to Michael. "Sure, what's up?"

"Max is one of your roommates, right?"

"Uh huh?" Caitlyn tilted her head. She didn't know what she expected Michael to ask, but she didn't expect that.

"Do you know if he..." Michael paused, considering. "Is he... seeing anyone?"

"What? Oh!" Caitlyn bit her lip. "I know he went out with some stage manager at another theater the other week, but I don't know if it was serious, or...well. Hmm. Tyler knows him better than I do, so maybe—" Another howl. She sighed. "Maybe I'll have a talk with Tyler and see what I can find out."

"Thanks, Cate. You're the best." Michael reached out to squeeze her shoulder. This time a panther screamed. They both turned to stare at the control booth. "Guess he's anxious to get going," Michael said.

"He's something," Caitlyn said.

She went to the dressing room to gather her belongings. When she didn't see Tyler waiting in the hall, she walked back to the stage. Everyone else appeared to have gone home. Only the work lights were on.

Something growled. Caitlyn rolled her eyes as she walked down the aisle to the control booth. "What the hell was that all about?"

"Who, me? What did I do?"

Caitlyn turned to glare at Tyler as he walked toward her. "You know exactly what you did," she said, gesturing at the booth. "You just did it again."

Another growl.

Her eyes widened as Caitlyn looked back and forth between Tyler and the control booth. "Wasn't me that time," he said, reaching for her hand.

"No shit."

Caitlyn and Tyler clung to each other as they ran back to the stage. They were almost at the back door leading to the hallway when a hulking, greenish-black shape with glowing eyes leapt in front of them. Caitlyn backed into a corner of the prop table and yelped. The beast's jaws opened in a menacing snarl, revealing wicked razor-sharp teeth.

"That's not a puppy," Caitlyn murmured.

It lunged.

twenty-five

* * *

On a whim, Caitlyn reached back to the prop table. With a triumphant shout, she lifted a prop sword and swung it at the beast's head as hard as she could. It felt like hitting a rock, but the beast yelped in surprise, shaking its head. Caitlyn dropped the sword, hand throbbing. Tyler took that opportunity to grab for her again, and they ran past the beast into the hall.

The beast was back on its feet, leaping after them. Now it was blocking the exit. They'd started to run the other way when the door behind them opened and a slender hand reached for Caitlyn, pulling her into a dressing room. She dragged Tyler back with her. Leanne pushed the door shut and began whispering strange words in a language Caitlyn didn't recognize. A strange shape briefly appeared on the door, glowing like it was on fire before disappearing. Outside, the beast whined and snarled.

"I'll hold it back as long as I can," Leanne said, looking the most focused Caitlyn had ever seen her. "But you need to calm down. It can sense your fear. It feeds on it."

"Are you crazy?" Tyler stared. "What is that thing? What are you?!"

Leanne didn't answer.

Caitlyn sat on the floor with her back against the wall. She reached up to tug at Tyler's pant leg. "I don't think it's the best time for twenty questions," she said. "Just let her do whatever it is she's doing. Maybe it'll get bored with us and go away."

Tyler sank to the floor beside her. Outside, the beast whined and scratched at the door. Something of that size should have had no problem breaking through, but whatever Leanne had said and done was keeping it at bay.

"You can think of it as a soul eater," Leanne said, turning to look at them.

"Is it the only one?" Caitlyn asked.

"In the building."

"But not the city," Caitlyn said. It wasn't a question.

Leanne's gaze lowered as confirmation.

"And it eats more than just souls," Tyler said. "It killed Billy."

Leanne nodded sadly. "I think so." She turned and listened at the door. "It's gone now. I don't think it will attack you in the street, but beware of any large dogs, especially if you find it hard to focus on their appearance for any length of time. There are other…beings…to look out for," Leanne said. "Some are smaller, more catlike. They steal your soul but leave your body as a mindless hollowed-out husk." She opened her mouth to say more, but then pressed her lips together. "There's so much I wish I could tell you. I just couldn't let anyone else die if I could help—"

"Leanne? Let's go!"

The strange woman appeared frightened when she heard Elliot's voice in the hall, even more frightened than she had been of the soul eater. "He can't know you're in here. Wait five minutes, then go. Tell no one of what you saw. For all of our sakes. Please?"

Caitlyn and Tyler nodded. Leanne opened the door. "I'm here." She stepped into the hall, closing the door behind her.

Tyler's eyes were wide. "Where do you suppose he was when all that was going on?"

"What the hell happened to you two? You look like you saw a ghost. Oh God, nobody else died, did they?" Max looked up from the sofa, where he was bundled under Caitlyn's rainbow leopard print blanket, eating a bowl of rice.

"There's some sort of massive hellhound stalking the theater," Caitlyn said, collapsing onto the couch beside Max. She was still shaking.

"A soul eater," Tyler said. "That's what Leanne called it." He sat across from them in the chair, his face morose as he stared at the wall across the room.

"Great. Yesterday there was mass food poisoning. Today it's mass hysteria." Max furrowed his brow. "Does the Blackstone Theater have gas heating?"

"We know what we saw, Max. It attacked us. Tried to, anyway. Caitlyn bonked it with a sword and then Leanne pulled us into her dressing room. She did something to the door, and it couldn't get in so it went away. Then Elliot called for Leanne and she left." Tyler turned to Caitlyn. "Don't vampires have dogs to protect them or something? I think I saw that in a movie once. Maybe Elliot was the vampire all along and it belongs to him."

"Then why would it kill Billy?" Caitlyn asked. "It doesn't benefit Elliot to sabotage his own show. Unless he really wants any publicity that he can get."

"Or maybe a stray dog got into the theater, and you're both so jumpy from the play and everything else that's been going on, you saw it as something worse than what it really was. As for Leanne, we already know she's weird. Oh shit, maybe one of those raccoons you've been carrying on about gave the dog rabies," Max said to Tyler. "Did either of you get scratched or bit or anything?"

Tyler looked bemused. "Not a lot of stray dogs roaming the city."

"I bruised my ass on a prop table. But the soul eater never touched me. Oh!" Caitlyn straightened. "Lloyd left a head in Maya's dressing room this morning!"

Max turned to Caitlyn, his eyes wide. "A real one?"

"No." Caitlyn deflated. "Just a prop head. It was a prank. Sort of trivial compared to everything else that happened, I suppose."

"Well, it supports my theory about everyone being extra-jumpy, anyway," Max said. "I suggest you two get some food in your stomach and call it an early night. Tomorrow we can get ahold of Manny and tell him about the dog."

Tyler looked like he was going to argue. Instead, he shook his head and walked to the cabinet to take out a couple packages of ramen.

"I was supposed to go out last night," Max told Tyler the next morning after Caitlyn left to meet Laurel at the ferry terminal. He could only hope Caitlyn had the sense not to tell anyone else about what she thought she saw last night.

"With that prop mistress?"

"Nah. Turns out we didn't have much to say outside of shop talk. But I've been texting back and forth with someone new." Max grinned. "A writer."

"When did that start?" Tyler looked surprised.

"You remember that night Caitlyn introduced us to her favorite sushi place?"

Tyler nodded.

"Well, you know how I didn't let Caitlyn pay for dinner? When I got my card back, the waitress had left me her number on the receipt."

"Wait, Carrie? Elliot's sloppy seconds?"

Max frowned. "Don't say it like that. Things never got that serious. She thought wanting to take it slow was why he blew her off. I guess he can be a little pushy. In small ways at first, but he'd play it off like he was just joking. Then it got worse, and when she was ready to break things off, he'd already moved on with Leanne."

"I hope you're not just using her for information," Tyler said.

"Of course not." Max rolled his eyes. "We talk about everything, just not…"

"Just not what?"

"The stuff happening at work, beyond the usual drama," Max said. "Oh, she knows all about Billy and Anne Marie. You can't walk by a newsstand and avoid those stories. We just talk about how wild the tabloid theories are. Vampires, hellhounds, all that bullshit."

"It wasn't some stray, Max. The thing was huge. Its fangs and its claws were as long as steak knives, and it had, like, this eerie green glow. But the crazy thing is, Leanne was even more afraid of Elliot than the soul eater."

Max chose to ignore the part about the soul eater as he looked at his frazzled friend. "It makes sense. We know he has a jealous streak. As far as I know, he never got violent with Carrie, but maybe things are worse between him and Leanne. We should probably be on the lookout for any signs of physical abuse. Wonder if I should broach that subject with Manny too."

"I dunno," Tyler said. "He was pretty wrecked about Billy. We should wait until we have something more solid to go on than gut instinct."

"Hi guys! Laurel has a theory." Caitlyn banged through the apartment door, ushering Laurel in behind her. Tyler looked up from his laptop, and. Max started to massage his temples, laying back on the sofa.

"Are you okay?" Caitlyn looked at him with concern. "I thought you were feeling better?"

"Yeah, great." Max gazed up at the ceiling, looking as world-weary as Caitlyn had ever seen him. "Never better."

"Okay, so anyway, tell 'em, Laurel."

Laurel gave Tyler a shy smile. "You know *The Hound of the Baskervilles*, right?"

Max sat up. "Tyler isn't big with classic literature."

"But I am big with streaming," Tyler glared. "I've seen the show. Sherlock Holmes?"

Laurel nodded. "It's based on old Gaelic lore about the Cú Sídhe."

Tyler blinked. "I'm sorry, the what now?"

"Cú means dog and Sídhe means fairy," Caitlyn said with authority. Laurel gave her an encouraging nod. "They eat people's souls. Oh, and there's also the Cait Sídhe. Leanne told us to watch out for strange cat-like things too, remember?"

"It wasn't a fairy dog in the novel." Max sighed. "Just a regular hound that the owner scared people into believing was supernatural."

Laurel frowned.

"He's not mad at you," Caitlyn assured her. "He's just not as open-minded about this sort of thing."

With a sympathetic tilt to her head, Laurel told Max. "I'm not sure what I believe." She turned to Tyler. "I just know there's all sorts of stories from all over the world dating back, well, ages. It's possible it all comes from the primal fears of prehistoric man, but maybe there's more to it. Matt's seen some strange things, too. Even Dad's favorite talk radio station has been talking about weird stuff. They're just blaming drugs or illegal immigration, though." Her frown deepened.

"We're meeting Jen and Cass for dinner before the show. Jen only has four tickets, but did you want to join us for dinner?" Caitlyn turned from Max and Tyler to Laurel. "We probably shouldn't mention the fairy dog. I don't think they're ready to hear it."

Max was rubbing his temples again.

Tyler looked worried. "What show?"

"*Moulin Rouge*. My first Broadway show, and we have front row seats in the mezzanine. I'm so excited." Caitlyn grinned.

Tyler relaxed. "Sounds like a safe wildlife-free environment, supernatural or otherwise. I'll pass on dinner. Have fun, though."

"I have a make-up date with a beautiful writer," Max said. "I can fill you in tomorrow."

Caitlyn nodded, furrowing her brow. "You do that."

Later that evening, Tyler looked up as Caitlyn walked into the apartment wearing another Cassidy-loaner, no doubt: a burgundy velvet dress with thin straps. She collapsed beside him on the couch with a dramatic sigh. "I need funny animal videos, stat." She wrapped her blanket around herself and leaned her head on his shoulder.

Tyler squirmed. She smelled like hair gel and perfume. He turned his attention to a different topic, hoping to distract himself.

"You knew she was going to die, right? Like, he says so right at the beginning of the movie."

"Yes, but I'm always hoping next time it will be different. Besides, this is the musical. They could have changed the ending," Caitlyn said. "Lightened it up a little."

Tyler wrinkled his nose. "I hate when Broadway takes all the bite out of movie adaptations." He started typing on his laptop. "What'll it be? Cats? Dogs?"

"Anything with fur. Or feathers. Scales." Caitlyn shrugged. "I'm not picky."

The door opened and Max walked in, looking rumpled with his shirt half untucked as he sat in the chair. "You got a little something on the corner of your mouth," Caitlyn told him. Looking rueful, Max wiped the lipstick away with the back of his hand.

Tyler smirked. "I take it you had a good date with Carrie?"

"Carrie?" Caitlyn looked between Tyler and Max. "Wasn't that the name of our waitress the other night? Is the stage manager a Carrie, too?"

"No, she was a Kimmy. This is the waitress."

"Elliot's ex," Tyler added.

Max gave him a withering stare. "It turns out we have a lot in common, and not just our mutual dislike of Elliot. Speaking of, it's safe to say he isn't a vampire—Carrie has been outside with him during the day—but he is definitely bad news. You should avoid being alone with him," he told Caitlyn.

"No problems there," Caitlyn said. "Group scenes only. Besides, it's all hands-on deck starting this week, right?" Max nodded. "So, I guess things are heating up between you and Carrie, huh? Because Michael was asking about you, and I didn't know what to tell him."

"Michael?" Max glanced at Tyler, looking amused. "He's a handsome man, beautiful in fact, but not really my type."

"Okay," Caitlyn said. "I didn't want to assume."

"Nope, there's a saying about that," Max said, smirking.

Tyler's ears burned.

twenty-six

. . .

"There was another article about our show in the paper this morning," Jordan told Caitlyn backstage on Monday morning. "Between dead techies, vanishing actresses, and the mass food poisoning, the writer said it's already looking like an even bigger disaster than some Spiderman musical years ago. Elliot's in more of a foul mood than he usually is. And Johnny's blocking the aerial stunt today." Her brow furrowed. "A death-free Monday. That's all I ask."

"I guess some people think it's just a big publicity stunt, but who wants bad publicity?"

"The only bad publicity is no publicity." Maya strode past them, smirking.

"At least someone's in a better mood today," Jordan said, watching the actress go.

Caitlyn raised an eyebrow. "Has anyone checked on Lloyd in his dressing room?"

Jordan glared. "A death-free Monday," she said, looking skyward. "I mean it."

. . .

"Oh, wow." Caitlyn considered the torn strips of cream-colored lace and sheer gauzy fabric that made up the skirt of her costume. A matching satin corset with chiffon off-shoulder straps completed her costume.

"Definitely won't want to skip leg day," Amelia said.

"I love it." Emma twirled.

Across the room, Susan was pinning Laurel's amethyst ball gown. "I think I've done some of my best work for this show," she said. The other women were dressed in similar gowns of various jewel tones—sapphire, emerald, topaz, all except ruby, no doubt reserved for Lucy. "Even the nurse and servant uniforms are darling."

Maya walked into the dressing room wearing an off-shoulder gown of dark red satin. Leanne followed in a more modest but no less beautiful gown of aquamarine accented with peacock feathers. For a moment, she looked so much like a porcelain doll, Caitlyn felt a chill run through her veins, and not just because of her scant costume. Whatever Leanne was, she was not of this world.

"Ah, perfect." Susan clapped her hands. "How do they feel?"

"Great," Maya said. "Should I try on the next costume?"

Susan nodded. After Maya left the room, she turned to Leanne. "How's yours? Does everything fit okay?"

"I'm worried I'll trip on the skirt," Leanne told her. "But it's beautiful."

"I'll be in to pin the skirt in a minute," Susan said. "The brides can get back into their street clothes, but the rest of you have one or two more pieces on the rack to try. Please help each other with zippers."

Elise yelped, putting an index finger in her mouth while Sophia bit her lip on a smile. "And watch out for pins," Susan said. "I should have adjustments made well ahead of your first dress rehearsal in a couple weeks."

Offstage, Jordan watched as Johnny blocked the boat scene, where Dracula comes to London from Transylvania. She held a finger to her lips as one of the women from the chorus walked over to watch—the one who bugged her about her brother last week. Steven removed his shirt so a couple of techies could help him into the rigging for the aerial stunt, revealing smooth brown skin and a slim muscular torso. *I don't spend* all *of my free time gaming,* he'd said last week when she grilled him about stunt work.

"Is he available?" Hailey stared at Steven.

Jordan sighed. "This is probably the most dangerous scene in the musical," she said. "I need to focus on work. Aren't you supposed to be learning your songs or your choreography or something?" Hailey flipped her curly black hair over her shoulder as she turned to walk away. Jordan looked back on stage just as Steven was lifted up to the catwalk. She held her breath until he sat down.

"How's everything feel?" Johnny looked up at the catwalk.

"It feels pretty secure," a techie called down. "What do you think?"

"I'm good," Steven said.

"Great. Now let's get him back down and run through the scene in its entirety." Johnny ran the techies and sailors through the scene several times until Elliot was satisfied with the blocking. Every time Steven was raised high above the stage, thrashing his legs and clawing at his neck as if someone was lifting him by the throat, Jordan's heart leapt into her throat. The other actors, Jack and Javier, jumped "overboard" instead—in reality, they were jumping into a couple of trap doors leading to safety pads below the stage. They would use sound and lighting to create the sea and storm effects.

"I still don't get what happened to the other prop sword," Luis said when he returned from the basement. "Looked like somebody swung it at a slab of concrete." He set the replacement sword on the prop table. "They finish the boat scene?"

Jordan nodded.

Luis nudged her shoulder. "Guess you were worried for nothing."

"Worrying keeps the bad things from happening," Jordan said.

"Now you're just being superstitious."

"Not really." Jordan rolled her eyes. "I anticipate what can go wrong, and I take steps to make sure it doesn't. That's why Amari and I went up on the catwalk to double check everything before rehearsal."

"Don't you trust Johnny or the other techies?"

"I trust double and triple checking."

．．．

Now that Emma was back, Elliot decided to run through the bedroom scene with Michael again. Amelia talked Emma into swapping starting positions so she could emerge from the shadows behind the bed instead of crawling up the stairs at the side of the stage. Elliot spent most of the time staring down at his phone and typing away, but he looked up once to praise Emma's performance. "Caitlyn, watch how Emma crawls onto the stage. She really nails the sexiness I'm going for. You still look like something out of *Night of the Living Dead.*"

Caitlyn pressed her lips together to keep from sneering.

"Hey," Luis said when she walked offstage, "if you want, I can rig something to make it look like you lose an arm or a leg on the way up the stairs. I think it'll give the scene that little extra something it's missing."

Caitlyn tried to glare but laughed instead.

"I dunno what Elliot's problem is," Luis said. "But I always had a little crush on I *Corpse Bride,* so I might be biased."

"Was it the forehead worm? I bet it was the forehead worm."

Now Luis laughed. "See you tomorrow, Catie-cat."

"Catie-cat?" Tyler asked when Caitlyn stepped into the hall.

"Yeah, I hate pet names," she said, "but I really like cats. It's a conundrum." In a lower voice, she added, "I tried talking to Leanne today, but she's been holed up in her dressing room whenever she isn't on stage."

"What else is new?" Max joined them. "Apart from Elliot being an even bigger creep than usual. Sorry for the way he was talking to you out there, Cait. I honestly don't think you looked any different than Emma did. It's like he has it in for you specifically."

"Maybe he knows we suspect something's up," Tyler said.

"Maybe he saw me that night at the club," Caitlyn said. "But he wasn't very nice to Amelia on Friday, either. She dodged a bullet swapping entrances with Emma. Maybe it's just Elliot being Elliot."

Even Max looked doubtful. "Maybe."

．．．

Apart from scene changes taking longer than Elliot liked—*what did he expect? It's the first run through of the first act!*—rehearsal was going well the following morning. Jordan slipped into a familiar rhythm of managing actors and techies as her brother assisted her with the curtains on the other side of the stage. Jordan didn't like Elliot, but she had to hand it to him—he'd assembled a great production team to bring his vision to life, and the cast was solid. Even the songs had grown more tolerable after a few rewrites, with Andre's input, she knew.

Matthew and Lloyd circled the center stage at the moment, with Matthew wearing a lab coat over his street clothes. For a creepy little dude, Lloyd had a great singing voice. That maniacal cackle, though.

Jordan cringed in anticipation of Lloyd pulling a worm from his coat pocket. They looked like the real thing now. No more green-and-red or yellow-and-orange gummies. Jordan didn't notice a problem right away when Lloyd sucked the worm into his mouth. Not until his eyes went wide—even by wild-eyed Lloyd standards—and he started to gag.

twenty-seven

. . .

Lloyd ran off stage and retched into a garbage can near Amari. "Ah, hell naw," Jordan heard her brother say. "That's messed up."

Matthew left the stage to help Lloyd.

Elliot stormed up the stairs to yell at Luis backstage. "What the hell happened? How did a real worm get into Lloyd's pocket?"

Bewildered, Luis held up the plastic ziplock bag of gummy worms to show Elliot. "I dunno," he said. "I handed one to him right from this bag. It's all gummies. Don't you think I'd notice grabbing a live worm?"

"Sorry to interrupt," came Max's voice over Jordan's headset, "but are we sure it was a real worm? Maybe he just swallowed wrong. Has anyone checked?"

"I ain't CSI," Amari protested.

Jordan sighed. "I'll look." she said. She walked across the stage to her brother, giving him a weary look of disgust before she glanced down into the garbage can. At least there wasn't any vomit, just chewed remnants of what looked like a gummy worm—a realistic gummy worm, but a gummy worm all the same. "Good call, Max."

"Set the next scene." Elliot glowered as he stormed off the stage.

. . .

"It wasn't a gummy worm," Matthew said, adjusting his glasses. "I saw it wriggle just before he put it into his mouth."

Laurel set her grilled cheese sandwich back down on her plate, frowning. She sat in a booth opposite Matthew at the diner by the Blackstone Theater. He had barely touched his BLT. And Matthew loved the diner's BLTs—with loads of mayo. Laurel could not decide which was more vomitous. Eating a live worm or lettuce and tomatoes drowning in mayo. She pushed aside her revulsion and reached across the table to give his hand an awkward pat.

"I bet it was Maya," Matthew said. "Not that I blame her. Messing with people's food isn't okay, though. I remember what happened that time you found lettuce in your sandwich."

Laurel looked down. She knew he meant it as a kind gesture or something benign, but she felt embarrassed just the same. "Sometimes people feel inspired to do all sorts of crazy things," she said. *Make a Broadway musical, play mean pranks, date someone new, consider moving away from the relative safety and security of home. Hmm.* She looked up, staring past Matthew. *The Fae can inspire people to do stuff, good and bad. They can even make them see things that aren't real. Except faeries aren't real, either.*

"I'm sorry," Matthew said. "I'm probably grossing you out. You've barely even touched your lunch and our break is almost over."

"We still have ten minutes," she told him. "It's fine."

"Poor Luis." Caitlyn shook her head as she trailed behind Max and Tyler after rehearsal. "Probably ruined worms for him."

Tyler stopped walking and turned to look at her, incredulous. "Poor Luis? He's not the one who ate a real worm."

"Nobody ate a real worm, remember?" Max said, still walking. "Apart from Lloyd's little freakout, you have to admit the day went pretty well," he said when Tyler and Caitlyn caught up to him. "It'll probably be smooth sailing from here on out. Well, as smooth as it can be with Elliot at the helm."

"There's already ads for the show in the paper," Caitlyn said as they reached the apartment building. "I can't believe we open in a few weeks. Laurel says our last dress rehearsal is on the eve of the Summer Solstice. Then it's opening night. She didn't know if it would be good or bad luck, though. Do you think we've sold any tickets yet?" She paused on the stairwell, chewing on her bottom lip.

Max and Tyler shrugged.

"Should I invite my dad to come see it?" Caitlyn asked as they continued climbing the stairs. "Maybe he should wait until the Broadway run. Plane tickets are so expensive. Do you think there'll be a Broadway run? What if people hate the show?"

"*I* hate the show," Max said. Tyler nudged his arm. "But the audience will love you." He reached out to squeeze Caitlyn's shoulder. "Try to relax."

The rest of the week was anything but relaxing as Elliot ran Act One of the show over and over again. Isabella had to rework some of the choreography for the ballroom scene in particular as the set came together, and Dracula and his brides had new lyrics to learn as James Merrick refined their songs.

"Not too bad," Andre said, looking down at the sheet of paper Diane handed to him Friday morning. "Did you say Leanne met with James?"

"And Elliot, obviously," Diane said. "I suppose he thought a pretty face might make James more receptive to everyone's notes and feedback. He has a reputation for being another one of those temperamental artist-slash-genius types."

"I dislike when people use the arts as an excuse to be abusive," Andre said. "So tiresome. How can we bring beauty and joy to the audience," he said, extending a hand to twirl a rapturous Emma into his arms, "if we do not bring it to each other?"

"I think he nailed the problem with a show meant to frighten people instead," Amelia said to Caitlyn in a low voice. "I wouldn't be surprised if putting the prop head in Maya's room was Elliot's idea. Probably planted a real worm, too."

"Maybe," Caitlyn said. "It's not like Jordan ran forensics on the evidence." She frowned. Somehow, even after her encounter with the soul eater, these mundane but mean-spirited pranks felt just as unsettling as everything else that had happened. Supernatural horrors were one thing; casual cruelty was another.

What if Elliot was just a man?

A man even someone as otherworldly and powerful as Leanne feared?

twenty-eight

. . .

"Somehow I've got to find a way to talk to Leanne," Caitlyn told Tyler Saturday morning as he joined her for one of her walks through Central Park. "Away from Elliot and the theater. I would've invited her to another girls' night out, but Jen and Cass are celebrating their anniversary, and Laurel's parents found out about Matt and invited him for dinner."

"If I was the religious sort, I'd say a quiet prayer for Matt," Tyler said.

"Seriously." Caitlyn paused to gaze at the statues outside the Delacorte Theater. "I know it's a lot different from musical theater, but I'd love to do Shakespeare in the Park someday. I think I'd rather do a comedy like *The Tempest* instead of something grim like *Hamlet* or the 'M' word, though."

"I think it's safe to say Ma…the name outside a theater, isn't it?" Tyler's brow furrowed. "On second thought, maybe we shouldn't tempt fate. Oof. That can't possibly be comfortable," he said, eyeing the statue of Romeo and Juliet locked in a passionate embrace.

Caitlyn bent backwards and lifted her arms to mimic Juliet's pose, to the amused stares of passers-by. Tyler watched, laughing, but rushed forward to help when she almost lost her balance. "My hero,"

Caitlyn said with a wry smile as Tyler helped to steady her, one hand pressing against her lower back and one on her arm.

Not sure what else to do, Tyler let go and took a step back, reaching a hand up to scratch the back of his neck. "We should probably head back to the apartment. I've got some data entry to catch up on," he said. *Was that disappointment in her eyes?*

Whatever it was, Caitlyn blinked it away. "No problem," she said, albeit with a note of false brightness in her voice.

Feeling bored and lonely, Caitlyn glanced in the direction of Max and Tyler's room. Max was out, presumably with Carrie, and Tyler was typing away on the bottom bunk instead of his own. He noticed her looking and raised a hand to wave. "Should be done with my work soon. Then we can order a pizza and find something to watch."

Caitlyn stretched out on the couch and looked at her phone. It rang as she was about to check her text messages. "Dad, hi, how are you?" She sat back up.

"How are *you*? I saw the strangest headline today, and I think they were talking about your show. A musical adaptation of *Dracula*, they said. Is it true that people have died?"

"Person," Caitlyn said. "One person. His name was Billy. Super-nice guy from what I've been told. It was sad." *And gross.* And *scary.* "But everything's fine now. We open in two weeks. Isn't that exciting? I thought about asking you to come visit, but maybe you should wait until the Broadway run, assuming there is one. I'm sure there will be. It's a great show."

"I'm sure it is, honey," her dad said. "Not sure if I can take time away from work just yet, but I'll be out to visit as soon as I can. I just wanted to make sure you were okay. How's the roommate search going?"

"Good, I think." Caitlyn frowned as she thought about the uncertainty of her plans with Laurel, Jennifer, and Cassidy. "I should know something in the next week or two."

"Glad to hear it. Take care of yourself. I love you."

"Okay. Love you, too."

As the call ended, Caitlyn sighed, staring down at her phone.

"I take it the news about the show has made it out of state?" Tyler walked out of the room and sat beside Caitlyn on the couch. "Is your dad going to come see it?"

"No." Caitlyn didn't look up.

Tyler nudged her shoulder with his own. "Do you miss him?"

"Yeah."

Tyler sat in silence with Caitlyn.

After a few minutes, she smiled at him and said, "What was that about pizza?"

"Already ordered."

"I wonder how Laurel's dinner is going." Caitlyn frowned again, her mind spinning. "She's supposed to talk to her parents about moving in with me, too. They seem way overprotective. What if they don't want her to move out?"

Tyler took Caitlyn's hand, squeezing it. "Laurel's a big girl. I'm sure she can handle it." He crossed his free hand behind his back.

"So, Matthew, do you have a backup plan?" Mr. Locke gave Matthew a stern look.

Laurel shot Matthew a look of sympathy as he choked down a dry piece of chicken.

"A backup plan?" His response came out garbled.

"Well, you don't expect to build a life for yourself acting, do you?" Mr. Locke pressed. "Laurel takes online courses at the community college. Any money she doesn't use for transportation goes to that, but she won't have time for any of this silly theater business once she transfers to a university."

"You won't apply for a fine arts program?" Matthew looked at Laurel in surprise.

"I was actually thinking of majoring in religious studies," Laurel said, hoping Matthew noticed the side-long glance she cast in her father's direction. Matthew opened his mouth to speak but closed it again. Laurel relaxed in her chair.

"Religious studies," Mr. Locke said. "Huh. Well, it's not STEM, but it sounds promising."

"I think I might move in with some nice women I know in the city, to save on transportation," Laurel ventured.

"As long as one of them isn't that strange flaky girl who visited the other weekend," Mr. Locke said. "She's trouble, you can tell." He exchanged a look with Mrs. Locke.

Her mother turned to Laurel. "Your father and I are worried for your safety. We've been hearing the most frightful stories. Drug busts. Human trafficking. Don't the universities have dormitories on campus? With security?"

Laurel sighed.

I swear they're like an old married couple and they're not even dating.

Max looked at his roommates curled up on the couch, sleeping. He closed Tyler's laptop and went to bed. Then he stared up at the ceiling, thinking about Carrie. She was smart and funny and totally at ease with him. Carrie felt less at ease with his working situation, but he had assured her that he rarely landed on Elliot's radar. Caitlyn was less fortunate, but the show was going live in less than two weeks, so their interactions would be less.

Still, he couldn't shake his own unease. It didn't help that Act Two had that big epic fight scene. So many prop weapons. A lot could go wrong there. Max had to remind himself that nobody had truly replaced Lloyd's gummies with the real thing. He felt his skin crawl when he considered worse possibilities. Max pushed them all out of his mind. He rolled over and went to sleep.

twenty-nine

. . .

"Places," Jordan called at the beginning of rehearsal on Monday. She could only hope Elliot had mentally prepared himself for another slog as the crew worked out the kinks of set changes. You couldn't rush these things. Not at first. Just one run-through of Act One had taken most of last Monday, but by the end of the week, they had it down to a tidy hour and a half.

On stage, Matthew attended to a bedridden Maya as Nicholas and Christopher looked on in concern, Christopher holding a cowboy hat against his chest. Leanne entered to comfort her sick friend and tell her of her own fiancé's return from Dracula's castle. The curtains remained open as the lights went down on their scene and the three men wheeled the bed offstage. Then the lights came up on another part of the stage to reveal Leanne and Michael for their duet.

So far, so good.

Later Johan, congenial offstage but intense and menacing as Van Helsing, made his grand entrance. Even without makeup and special effects—those would be introduced later this week—Maya was terrifying as a transformed Lucy. Christopher and Matthew pulled her away from a spellbound Nicholas, and Johan held up a cross as he forced her back into her coffin. Nicholas serenaded her one last time before "dispatching" her with his sword.

To everyone's surprise, Elliot rose in the audience and applauded. Maya sat up in her coffin, raising an eyebrow as she eyed Elliot with suspicion. His mirth appeared genuine to Jordan. "Bravo, everyone. Bravo, Maya. Still some kinks to work out, but now seems like a good time to break for lunch, and then we'll finish the rest of Act Two. I don't know about the rest of you, but I can't wait to see the final fight on a completed set."

Johan held out a hand to help Maya from the coffin and congratulated her on her performance. She smiled as she gushed over his own performance.

Even Andre emerged from the shadows to praise the group, having traded in his costume for street clothes. "I couldn't resist sneaking a peek," he said. "Never have I had the pleasure of working with such a fine group of performers. I, too, look forward to our fight." He winked and left the stage with Johan.

Jordan removed her headset and battery pack and placed them on her chair. She did not share everyone else's enthusiasm for the upcoming fight scene, but for now she took comfort in Elliot's improved attitude. Maybe the director finally had trust in his cast and crew. They'd more than earned it. Most of them, anyway. Jordan still felt a little shaky about Lloyd, even if she pitied the actor after last week's scare.

For his part, Luis had become even more diligent in managing his props. "Careful," Jordan had teased him earlier that morning, "you're turning into an anxious mother hen, just like me."

"What can I say?" he'd said, grinning. "You inspire me."

Steven caught up with Jordan in the hallway. "Some of the guys are getting pizza, but I'm sick of it. Wanna grab lunch next door?"

Jordan smiled. Her brother could fend for himself today.

Caitlyn glanced offstage to make sure she wouldn't back into anything when Christopher drove her offstage with his prop sword in a few moments. Elliot had decided the three vampire brides would be dispatched in the wings to save the most dramatic ending for Dracula. Jordan looked tense as she watched the fight scene play out, and even Luis looked on edge. Caitlyn refocused and hissed at the actors on stage.

She descended upon Christopher with Emma and Amelia. No blood bags today, but they would leave his character mortally wounded. Matthew and Nick pulled Emma and Amelia off Christopher. He stumbled after Caitlyn with his retractable sword, then plunged it into her stomach. Caitlyn mewled as she backed away. All the audience would see was Christopher removing the sword and swinging it in her direction.

Caitlyn stood in the wings to watch the rest of the scene. Emma and Amelia smiled and waved from the opposite wings. She gave them a thumbs up and watched as Nick and Matthew attended to Christopher. Michael and Johan advanced on Dracula: Johan with his crucifix, Michael with his sword. Elliot had decided weeks ago not to involve Leanne in the final fight because it was a departure from the book that carried less weight without an inflated romance between Mina and Dracula.

The new and improved fight between Michael and Andre resembled a dance. Johnny and Isabella had worked together to create something thrilling and beautiful. Caitlyn's heart leapt into her throat as Michael gained the upper hand and forced Andre into the shadows. He raised his sword and swung. Andre looked genuinely surprised as he reached for his throat and—wait, wasn't he supposed to stumble behind the pillar?

And was that real blood?

Michael dropped the sword and rushed to Andre's side.

A palled Luis walked on stage and reached for the sword as Johan and Michael helped Andre offstage. More flurry of movement as Jordan ran to Luis and Elliot walked up the steps. Luis touched the edge of the sword. "It's blunt," he confirmed, looking mystified.

. . .

"I could swear I saw blood," Caitlyn told Max and Tyler as they walked home after Elliot called it an early night. Andre had been shaken up, but was otherwise uninjured, and Michael felt horrible. Elliot and Johnny decided to rework the last part of the fight scene to minimize the chance for contact. Blunted or not, getting hit with a prop sword didn't tickle.

"You gotta admit, it's pretty weird people had another shared hallucination," Tyler said to Max. "Caitlyn wasn't the only one who saw blood."

"And it happened on a Monday, just like last time," Max said, his eyes wide. "Clearly Mondays are cursed."

Tyler opened his mouth to speak, then pressed his lips back together, giving Max an annoyed look. "Look, I'm just saying a lot of weird things have been going on in the city, and the theater seems like a focal point for most of them."

"That we know," Caitlyn said, thinking about the dead things in Central Park and all the disappearances involving The Way Station. She shivered.

"I don't think you two are a good influence on each other," Max said.

Tyler looked agitated, and Caitlyn frowned.

"Oh, don't be like that." Max nudged her arm with his own. "We're all worn down, and it's starting to get to us. That's all."

On Tuesday, hair and makeup came in to start working with the cast on creating their looks. Candy Clark, a large busty woman with bright blond hair and a big smile, led the team. "Such a glum group," she said when she came into the dressing room with a few other women, all armed with makeup bags, curling irons, and other tools of the trade. "You're going live next week. Aren't you excited?"

Caitlyn couldn't help but grin at the makeup artist's enthusiasm. It was contagious. Almost enough to make the rest of the production seem less cursed.

"For you," Candy said when she consulted with the three vampire brides, "I think we're going to airbrush a clown white base. A little bit will go a lot further, and you won't have that awful cakey look." Caitlyn stood patiently as Candy started with her. Across the room, another hair stylist and makeup artist worked with the other women.

"I like it," Emma said after everyone's hair and makeup was done. Her tousled auburn locks fell down her back in wild curls. "It's got that freshly fu—" she started to say before glancing in Laurel's direction. "Freshly you-know-what'd look."

"My hair never looked this good after sex," Amelia said.

"I'd question how good the sex was if it did," Sophia said from across the room. Everyone laughed.

"Now, that's what I like to see and hear," Candy said. "Everyone smiling and laughing." She walked to the door. "Y'all behave now," she said. "But not too much."

"Never," Emma called after her.

Rehearsal went much better after Andre's scare on Monday, and even Jordan appeared more relaxed as the week went on. "I'm starting to wonder if Mondays really are cursed," Max said to Tyler as they left the control booth.

"Don't say that." Tyler made a face. "Our first full run-through with tech is Monday night. After that, there's just two more rehearsals. Then we go live."

"Well," Max said, "at least the show only runs Thursdays through Sundays. Assuming it doesn't tank and they cancel the show altogether."

"Why would the show get canceled?" Caitlyn's eyes were wide when she caught up with them in the aisle. "Did you hear something? I was supposed to get together with everyone this weekend to start talking about rent and stuff. Cass and Jen's roommate moves out next week."

Tyler sighed. "The show isn't getting canceled. Max is just being his usual upbeat self."

"Don't scare me like that," Caitlyn said to Max.

"How else would you like me to scare you?"

Caitlyn huffed. Max laughed.

Something small skittered through the row of chairs behind them, but they didn't hear it, not even when it caught up to something else and chattered at it. The *something else* chattered back, and then both skittered between the seats, into a dark crevice near the stage.

thirty

. . .

"Hey, sis?" Jordan looked across the stage at her brother as he talked into his headset. "It looks like something chewed some of the wood holding up a flat. It's about to topple over."

"Must be Monday." She sighed. "I'll send someone to fix it. In the meantime, Max needs someone to go with him onto the catwalk to make sure everything is secure. Tyler's tracking down extra mics because Nick managed to drop his and step on it."

"Some of these actors are a pain," Amari said.

"You've learned so much," Jordan said. She turned and bumped into Luis.

"I swear, nothing is ever where I left," he said, glaring down at the prop table.

"First day in the theater?"

Luis rolled his eyes. "I'm always the last to leave besides you and Elliot. Are *you* moving my stuff around?"

"Of course not," Jordan said. "Sort it out. Elliot wants a clean run-through, with dinner to coincide with intermission. And I do not want to be here all night. Gonna be a long week as it is." *And minimal downtime to take the edge off with Steve.*

"Yeah, yeah." Luis returned to straightening up his prop table.

"What a grouch," Jordan said. "I love tech week." She sighed as she headed for the orchestra pit to make sure the conductor and musicians didn't need any more music stands or water. More proverbial cats to herd. Such fun.

"Tech week is the worst," Caitlyn said to her castmates when they had their dinner break almost an hour later than planned. "First the orchestra blew our cue. Then Luis snapped at me for knocking something off the prop table by mistake. And he called me Caitlyn."

Emma raised an eyebrow. "That's your name, isn't it?"

"Yes, but he usually calls me Catie-cat. It's, like, our thing. Never mind."

"We're not even getting a full week before we go live," Amelia said. "We still have sets falling apart and props disappearing. And don't even get me started on everything happening at the rest home. Someone else died over the weekend. It wasn't that unexpected, but my grandmother is freaking out."

"Is she coming to see you?" Caitlyn looked at Amelia with concern.

"Her whole building is. Well, some of the staff and any of the healthier residents, anyway." Amelia brightened. "I'm working with the rest home to set up a field trip to one of our Sunday matinee performances. I'm still waiting to hear back on group rates. Though I find myself wondering if a horror musical is the best idea, all things considered…" Amelia trailed off.

"I've been telling everyone I know," Emma said. "And I heard opening night is close to selling out. It can only get better once people see how great the show is."

"You know, it doesn't look half bad." Tyler told Max as he watched the actors sparring onstage. "It's all coming together pretty well. When rats aren't chewing up the set anyway."

"And we haven't had any major catastrophes tonight. So you know Elliot must be stoked."

"Don't jinx it." Tyler sat up as Michael approached Andre with a raised sword. Now Andre disappeared into the shadows completely with some clever rearranging of the stage and lighting adjustments by Max. Johan reached down and lifted the prop head. Tyler let out a low whistle. It looked pretty convincing from the control booth.

Max brought the lights down and back up as Elliot gathered the performers on stage to set up the curtain call. He yawned, rubbing at his eyes. "Kind of a boring night," he said, "but after the last few weeks, I'll take it."

———

Tuesday's rehearsal went better than Monday's. No missed cues or backstage accidents. After finishing her dinner, Caitlyn decided to take advantage of the relative peace and quiet to check on Leanne, but Elliot caught up with her in the hallway before she could knock on the dressing room door.

"Caitlyn, I just wanted to let you know that you've been doing a great job the past few days," Elliot said. "I know I've been really hard on you lately, but it's only because I want to help you meet your potential," he said.

Though his words seemed friendly enough, something about Elliot's stance made Caitlyn wonder if he knew where she was trying to go and why. "Thanks, Elliot. That means a lot." Her eyes flitted to Leanne's door. She could tell he saw. "I just wanted to see if Leanne wanted to hang out. I've noticed she never eats with the rest of the cast."

Elliot placed a gentle but firm hand on Caitlyn's elbow and led her away from the door. "Leanne has a strong commitment to her craft," he said. "She doesn't like distractions. You'd be wise to follow her example." His eyes returned to their usual cold and dispassionate state. "We begin Act Two in less than five minutes."

With a sigh, Caitlyn returned to her own dressing room to prepare for the second act. Still, she wondered. If anyone had any insight into strange happenings here and around the city, Leanne would. More importantly, Caitlyn suspected she needed a friend.

thirty-one

. . .

"I think there's rats in the orchestra pit," a flutist told Jordan on Wednesday.

"Right now?"

The flutist grimaced. "No, just in general. I saw weird claw marks on the floor, and my stand was moved over to the right when I came in."

Jordan raised an eyebrow.

"And sometimes we hear things running around, like they're inside the walls?"

Jordan shrugged. "I can talk to the building's manager about getting an exterminator out again. Just make sure nobody brings any food down there. Waters only."

Jordan assumed her position in the wings as the rest of the musicians filtered in and walked down into the orchestra pit. Luis double checked his props. Across the stage, Amari spoke to some stagehands and pointed to this set piece and that, giving directions. He was a quick study, she had to give him that—even though Amari insisted he had no interest in the theater world beyond making some extra money over the summer.

. . .

Laurel's favorite part of the show was the ballroom scene—not just because it was her biggest number or because she got to wear a beautiful amethyst dress of satin and chiffon that looked so amazing whenever she spun across the stage—but because of her moments spent partnered with Matthew. He always had a special smile just for her, even after that uncomfortable family dinner last weekend.

Her father hadn't liked Matthew even though her mother tried—briefly—to defend him. He wasn't a fan of Caitlyn either. But Laurel had realized she didn't need his approval. She was an adult. She had her own income. She could move in with three other women if she wanted. Laurel had left out the nature of Jennifer and Cassidy's relationship. She just wanted her freedom. She didn't need to give the grumpy old man a coronary.

Laurel grinned at Caitlyn waiting in the wings as Nicholas passed her to Christopher during the quickstep, then smiled up at Matthew when they finished the number together. She was surprised when Elliot paused the rehearsal to yell at the performers for what he felt was a sloppy performance. "And wipe that stupid grin off your face."

That was to Laurel. Her cheeks burned, and Matthew gave her hand a reassuring squeeze. "Ignore him," he whispered in her ear.

"Elliot's an ass," Jennifer said, patting Laurel's shoulder as they went backstage.

Shame whatever killed that poor techie hadn't attacked Elliot instead. Laurel felt startled by the intensity of her hatred for the bullying director. Now she heard him directing his rage at Caitlyn and the other brides. Her guilt dissipated.

"You know," Jordan said to Luis between set changes, "it's kind of sweet the way Elliot brings the cast and crew together."

Luis snorted.

Jordan watched as stagehands helped Steven into his harness for the ship scene. He looked up at Jordan as he buttoned his shirt over it and smiled. She forced a smile in return.

Jordan didn't relax until the scene ended and Steven descended back to the stage. The final scene of Act One was Dracula seducing

Lucy. Their number always gave Jordan chills. When the scene ended and the stage went dark, it took Jordan a moment to realize that *everything* had gone dark. She sighed. *Of course, the power would go out during their final dress rehearsal. Of* course.

Elliot was not amused. "Isn't there a backup generator?"

"Did you hear that?"

"Hear what?" Max squinted at Tyler in the darkness. His roommate stared at the ceiling.

"Sounds like someone's moving around up there."

"Doubtful," Max said. "Elliot decided he doesn't want to use the spotlight at all for this show." He felt the hair on his arms rise. "Wait. I hear something, too."

"Should we see if Jordan needs help?"

Tyler didn't have to ask twice.

Max reached for his flashlight and followed Tyler out of the control room.

Someone knocked on the men's dressing room door. "You decent?" came a female voice.

"Everyone's dressed," Christopher called out, "if that's what you mean."

Jordan pushed the door open and poked her head in. She was wearing her headset and holding a flashlight. "We don't know why the backup generator didn't kick in, but someone is on their way. It's just the theater. The rest of the block is fine. Elliot is giving it another twenty minutes or so, and he'll decide from there." She left.

Christopher looked around the dressing room. Everyone's faces were lit by their phones, except for Michael, who appeared to be meditating from his still but relaxed silhouette. Nicholas glanced up from his phone and said, "So whatever happened with you and Cait? Weren't you going out or something?"

"Just the once," Christopher said with a shrug.

"Didn't do it for ya, huh?"

"It was our first and only date." Christopher sighed. "She's awesome, but I got the sense she wasn't emotionally available, you know?"

Nicholas gave him a blank stare that said *no, no he did not.* "So that whole southern gentleman routine isn't just an act?"

"Some people save the acting for the stage, Nick," Michael spoke up.

A few moments of merciful silence, then: "I think I'm starting to grow on Maya."

"Have you ever considered *not* dating a costar?" Javier asked. The quiet dancer usually avoided weighing in, but even a laid-back guy like Javier had his limits, Christopher supposed.

"What, like a techie?" Nicholas grimaced. Then he tilted his head, considering. "Jordan's kind of hot."

Steven gave Nicholas a dubious look. "Jordan can see right through your ass." He looked back down at his phone. "So can Maya, no doubt."

"What do you think they talk about in the other dressing room?" Jack asked Matthew.

Matthew shrugged. "Laurel doesn't like to gossip," he said.

"Probably their feelings," said Nicholas, sounding sage.

"Anybody wanna play MFK?" Hailey's voice broke the silence.

"What?" Laurel recognized Emma's voice nearby.

"MFK? You in?"

"Oh!" A pause. "My 'Marry' is Andre, but you all already know that. Hmm. I dunno…maybe Nick?"

"Ew." That came from Laurel's immediate right. Jennifer.

"Look, he's not my usual type, but it's not like the game's asking who I want for deep and meaningful conversation," Emma said. "I'd consider giving him a test run, just to see what all the fuss is about. For science."

Someone laughed. Sophia?

"Girl, you better make sure he wraps it," Hailey advised.

"Obviously." Emma retorted, and Sophia broke out in giggles

again.

More laughter from the group. "Sophia, if you don't hush up with that, you're gonna be Elise's 'kill,' and there won't be any witnesses," Amelia said. "Can't see shit."

"Could I call dibs on Elliot?" Laurel surprised herself by blurting out.

"If he's your 'kill,' you're gonna have to get in line behind Maya and Caitlyn and, like, half the crew," Emma said. "He *is* your 'kill,' right?"

"Of course," Jennifer said. "She's with Matt-oof! God, Cass, what? Is it a secret?"

"Laurel and Matthew, huh…" Emma said in a thoughtful voice. Even in the dark, Laurel sensed it as the mood tensed. "Gah…that's so cute. I love it!"

"I swear," Hailey grumbled. "Everybody's gettin' some but me." Her face lit up in the darkness as she opened her phone. "Already half past nine. Elliot better let us go if the power doesn't come back any time—"

"Shh." Amelia's brow furrowed. "Does anyone hear that?"

Laurel listened. "Sounds like growling."

———

Caitlyn used to think the most terrifying thing that could happen in the bathroom was the toilet failing to flush under less-than-ideal circumstances, but she'd never had the power go out when she was in a public restroom before. "Shouldn't there be, like, emergency lights or something?" she muttered to herself. She reached for her phone but fumbled with it in the darkness. It clattered to the floor with an unmistakable cracking sound.

Caitlyn whimpered, struggling to remember if she was due for a replacement under her father's plan. Doubtful. She broke a phone last year, too. A new phone would be at least a couple weeks' pay. What a nightmare.

Caitlyn knelt down and felt around for her phone. Tyler's theory that the bright yellow case would glow in the dark did not appear to be valid. "Ouch!" She almost brought her bleeding finger to her mouth, then remembered where she was. "Great, now I'm gonna get sepsis or something." Caitlyn heard a thud and then movement in the stall behind her.

The sound of sharp claws against linoleum, followed by a low growl.

Caitlyn ran.

She hoped she was running in the right direction, swearing as she bumped a corner of the sink on the way out. Another door opened, and Leanne pulled her into her dressing room. "We have got to stop meeting like this," Caitlyn said as Leanne murmured in that strange language of hers to seal the door. As her eyes adjusted to the darkness, Caitlyn peered at Leanne's face. "Is it after you?"

"I don't know," Leanne said. "I don't think so." She looked away from Caitlyn to stare at the door. "I just know that it's not supposed to be here. None of them are. They must be coming through an unauthorized vortex somewhere. The park, maybe?" Leanne wasn't even talking to Caitlyn anymore.

And what the hell did she mean by an unauthorized vortex?

"You're not from around here, are you?"

Leanne turned to Caitlyn. "You can't know any of this," she said. "It isn't safe."

"Did Anne Marie find something out? Is that why she's gone?"

Even in the dark, Caitlyn could tell from Leanne's crestfallen face that the answer was yes. "I was lonely," Leanne said. "I...I just wanted a friend. We're supposed to make friends. It's how we blend. And he used it against me. He uses everything against me. My sister..."

Leanne started to say more but someone knocked on the door. Caitlyn realized she hadn't heard the soul eater since Leanne had pulled her into the dressing room. Was their nightmare finally coming to an end?

Leanne didn't seem to think so. She backed away from the door until her back was against the far wall. "It's him," she whispered. "Elliot."

"So?"

Caitlyn strode to the door, ready to give Elliot a piece of her mind.

She didn't know what Leanne was, but Elliot was just a man. A bully. She knew that now.

Besides, what was he gonna do?

Hit her?

Before Caitlyn could reach for the knob, Elliot pushed the door open. She squinted at him in the darkness as he raised something over his head and brought it down on her skull so swiftly she heard a whoosh of air before she saw stars. "Ow," Caitlyn said, surprised. She reached for her forehead and felt a trickle of blood above her temple. Then she fell to the floor.

thirty-two

. . .

As the lights came back on, Laurel took a deep, shaky breath. She must have imagined the growling—it was probably just her nerves—but there had been some sort of commotion in the hall. Techies tripping over each other, no doubt. Still, she felt her brow furrow as she met Amelia's gaze.

"Where's Cate?" Amelia said to Laurel, worry on her face.

"Uhm, I think she said she was going to the bathroom," Jennifer said. "Just before the power went out."

"Maybe that was Cait we heard bumping into things," said Cassidy.

Laurel rose and walked out of the dressing room. "Cait? Catie, where are you?" She looked up and down the hallway, then walked toward the restroom. A door opened behind her.

"Maybe she's in Leanne's room. I could have sworn I heard talking," Maya said. "But I heard a lot of other sounds, too." She frowned, then walked to Leanne's room and knocked on the door. Nobody answered.

Laurel gave her a worried look before going into the restroom. It appeared to be empty, but when she looked down at the floor, she saw a smartphone with a shattered screen. It had a neon yellow case, so it was harder to lose and easier to find—Laurel remembered Caitlyn telling her that. She pulled out a paper towel from the dispenser to pick up the phone, careful to avoid the broken screen.

Tyler and Max were waiting in the hall when Laurel walked out. Emma held open the door of the dressing room with the other women clustered behind her. Other doors opened as the men came out of their dressing rooms.

"Did you find Cait?"

Laurel shook her head at Tyler and held out Caitlyn's phone for him to see.

"Elliot's calling it a night," Jordan said, walking into the hall. "I guess he was satisfied with last night's run through of the second act. Rest up, everyone. Tomorrow, we o—" Jordan paused. "What's wrong?"

"Cait's missing," Max told her.

"So's Leanne," Maya said, leaning against the wall between her dressing room and Leanne's. "Or at least she isn't opening her door."

Jordan walked past her and knocked, then twisted the doorknob. Leanne's room was empty.

"Okay. Elliot can worry about his girl. I'll help you look for Cate before we lock up," she told Max and Tyler. "The rest of you, go home."

The cast members exchanged confused and worried looks but started to leave. Laurel hesitated.

"I mean it," Jordan said, putting a hand on Laurel's shoulder. "If she's still here, we'll find her."

"And if she isn't?"

Jordan didn't have an answer to that.

thirty-three

. . .

"So, your roommate has only been missing since last night?"

Max returned the officer's disinterested stare with an exasperated one of his own. He stood with Tyler in front of a desk in the precinct closest to their apartment. "She wouldn't just run off from the theater without telling anyone," he said. "The three of us always walk home together. Always."

"What theater did you say this was?"

"The Blackstone Theater." Tyler's anxiety was palpable, so Max had done most of the talking until now. "Maybe you've heard of it?"

The officers exchanged bemused glances. "Look," said the first, "as long as she hasn't been found bleeding in the rafters, it's too soon to worry about foul pla—"

"I'd like her found before it comes to that," Max interrupted.

"Just fill out the form," the officer said with a note of finality in his voice.

Max took the paperwork and sat in a chair beside Tyler. "You don't even have to wait a full twenty-four hours to report adults missing anymore. After Anne Marie and Billy, you'd expect a little more urgency," he said in a low voice. "And as far as I'm concerned this whole damn musical is a foul play."

"I'm glad you still got jokes at a time like this." Tyler scowled.

"I'm dead serious." Max winced. "I shouldn't have said 'dead.' I'm sorry."

"I don't think she's dead," Tyler said, "but she would not miss opening night unless something was very seriously wrong. Max, what are we going to do?" He ran his hands through his hair, which had grown so wild and unruly that he was starting to resemble Lloyd.

Max refrained from telling him so. "I don't know," he said instead.

A groggy Caitlyn pushed herself into a sitting position. She prodded the swollen goose egg over her brow with one hand. It felt tender to the touch, and there was a little bit of dried blood and a thin scab.

"What's he gonna do? Hit me?" she asked herself, sighing. "You *dumbass*."

Caitlyn looked around, considering her surroundings. She appeared to be in a basement—a finished one, thankfully—with hardwood floors and random pieces of furniture and typical basement stuff like paint and unused carpet neatly stacked against a wall. A little bit of dust. Not a lot of cobwebs. Light streamed in through a high window at what Caitlyn assumed was ground level. She wasn't in the city anymore. That much she knew.

Fabulous.

Caitlyn heard a rustle of movement. She turned and noted the king-sized bed in the corner with surprise. A dark-haired figure in a nightgown rose.

"Leanne?"

The woman stepped closer. Not Leanne. She had the same dark hair and eyes, but Leanne didn't have skin so translucent the veins gave her an eerie blue glow like the woman standing in front of Caitlyn. Or if she did, she was even better with makeup than Cassidy was. Caitlyn had seen skin like this before, but where?

The Way Station!

As the woman took another step closer, her lips curled up into a wicked smile. Now was *not* the time for a trip down Memory Lane.

Caitlyn rose to her feet and started backing away. "You're Leanne's sister, right?"

Leanne did say she had a sister, didn't she?

"I'm her friend."

And we don't eat sisters' friends, okay?

"It's not so bad if you don't fight it," said a new voice. Caitlyn looked past Leanne's sister to see another figure sitting up in the bed. A too-thin blonde in a rumpled red cocktail dress. Even though her hair was limp and tangled, and her blue eyes had lost their malevolent spark, Caitlyn still recognized her.

"Anne Marie? Oh my god—are you okay?"

Anne Marie looked like the world's most unfortunate stray as she tilted her head and furrowed her brow. "Anne Marie? Is that who I am? I'd forgotten…"

Leanne's sister had moved in close enough to caress Caitlyn's arm. "Ugh. This is so creepy," Caitlyn said. The woman didn't seem to take offense as she nuzzled Caitlyn's neck. "Are you a vampire? Will it hurt?"

"I don't bite," Leanne's sister said, pouting. *That* offended her. She reached up to cup Caitlyn's chin with her slender fingers. "I can inspire you to greatness, and all I need in return is just the teeniest bit of your life force. It's more than a fair trade, I think."

"Oh, is that all?" Caitlyn stiffened when Leanne's sister leaned in to kiss her on the lips, feeling herself relax as she closed her eyes and drifted into some sort of dream state. *Roommate or not, I should lay one of these on Tyler,* she found herself thinking. Caitlyn leaned into the kiss, opening her eyes in surprise and disappointment when it ended.

Leanne's sister gave her a sly smile, reminding Caitlyn of a cat toying with its food.

"That is *so* not okay," Caitlyn said. "Can Leanne do that, too?"

Leanne's sister frowned. "She doesn't like to. It's why they let her come. She has control. But I don't want to control it. Why should I?" Her cat-like grin returned. "It's not so bad, is it?"

Have you seen *Anne Marie?*

"She's a captive," Leanne's sister said, shrugging. "I don't think Elliot feeds her enough. But he takes good care of me. My sister wanted to keep me hidden away. At least Elliot takes me out to play now and then, as long as I look the part." Her skin turned creamy and opaque. Caitlyn could see the similarity to Leanne up close. From a distance, they could be twins.

"Okay," Caitlyn said. "First of all, thoughts are private. If I want you to hear me, I'll speak out loud. And people don't like being fooled or manipulated." Caitlyn paused. "Most people, anyway. And I don't think you like Elliot calling the shots, either. We should help each other find a way out of here."

"You can veil your thoughts from me all you want," Leanne's sister said in a darker, less kittenish tone, "but you and I both know hunters will find anyone who doesn't belong here. In both of our worlds."

For the first time in a long time, Caitlyn remembered the man she had encountered on the subway. His hunt had cost him his job. "Yeah, well, I don't think you have too much to worry about when it comes to the hunters from my world," she said. "They don't target women who look like you and your sister–well, when you're not all blue and veiny, anyway."

"Do you think he's already here? Call isn't until five."

"He's here," Max said to Tyler as he pushed open the back door. "Manny messaged to complain that Elliot's driving him up the wall, even more so than usual. After everything that's happened, he can't afford for anything else to go wrong. Especially on opening night."

They found Leanne standing in the hallway, looking lost as always. She was still in her street clothes, a floral sundress. When she saw them, she ducked into her dressing room and closed the door. Max wanted to talk to her but suspected Elliot wouldn't like that.

"You have to admit she doesn't belong here," Tyler said.

"In the theater world maybe," Max said, "but I'll never believe she's not of this earth."

They found Elliot sitting in the business office, tapping a pen on the desk and looking even more agitated than usual as he gazed at the lack of a view in the back alley. A creature scurried past, and Elliot's face darkened. He looked up as Max and Tyler stepped into the office. "Call isn't until five," he said.

"Have you seen Cait?" Tyler knew Max wanted to take a more cautious approach with Elliot, but he couldn't help but be direct. "She's been missing since last night's rehearsal."

"I don't have time to deal with anymore flaky actresses." Elliot slammed his pen down and rose from his chair, pointing his finger at Max and Tyler in turn as he continued speaking. "If she's not here by five, the show goes on without her—until we can recast and prepare someone else to take over her role. But she can forget about acting in this town ever again."

"Yes, sir," Max said hurriedly.

Tyler felt surprised at his friend's deferential tone but followed Max out of the office. He looked back at Elliot, but the director had sat back down, staring sullenly out the window once more.

"And the Tony award goes to…" Max said once they were outside.

Tyler raised an eyebrow. "Seemed plenty angry to me."

"Oh, he's angry all right," Max said. "He also knows something."

Tyler's eyes widened as he stared past Max. "I think that guy knows something, too."

A man in a dark suit and glasses stood in the shadow of the neighboring building, staring at them. Tyler remembered Caitlyn's description of the man she saw at Coney Island. This had to be the same guy.

thirty-four

. . .

As the morning waned on, Caitlyn was no closer to finding a solution to her captivity—though she had learned Leanne called her sister, of all things, Babs. Maybe the nickname was short for Babette, but that sounded just as ridiculous. Whatever her real name was, Babs had assured Caitlyn she'd never be able to say it.

"I don't know why you're wasting all your energy pacing back and forth," Babs said, her expression mild as she watched Caitlyn from the bed. "Elliot won't be back until much later tonight. Not until after his silly little show."

At least that meant she had to be somewhere close to the city. Maybe she was in Yonkers. Caitlyn snorted. *Trapped in Yonkers with Babs the succubus vampire-fairy whatever-the-fuck. Why not?* Caitlyn's amusement gave way to a new wave of grief when she remembered Elliot's silly little show was *her* silly little show, too. Opening night, and she was going to miss it. Somehow that felt like the biggest affront of all—not the head injury and potential for more pain and suffering, even death, but losing her first real chance at a big break.

"You should lay down," Anne Marie said. "I like dreaming. Dreaming is better." She gazed around the dusty basement, looking even more morose than Caitlyn felt. "So much better than this." She appeared to take her own advice as her head fell back against the pillow. "I'm going to be a star," she said with a sweet smile, closing her eyes.

"*Of course* you are, dear." Babs patted Anne Marie's thigh.

Caitlyn rolled her eyes.

"Are you okay?" Tyler asked Max.

"Sure," Max said, staring into space as he sank into the chair in their apartment. "Great, never better." He turned to Tyler. "You know, I always figured Leanne wasn't from around here, but I just thought she was, like, Canadian or something. Oh, and there really are men in black, but they're not from around here, either."

"It's a lot," Tyler agreed. "At least we get to keep our memories and stuff. I guess it's not like we can tell anyone else what we know. They'd ship us off to a loony bin for real."

"I just wish we knew what to tell that guy—or whatever he is— about Cate," Max said.

"Sounds like he has a lead, anyway," Tyler said. "Now all we can do is sit and wait and hope he finds her before showtime."

"There're more important things than a stupid musical," Max said.

"Not to Cate."

At some point Caitlyn had fallen asleep in a lumpy old armchair with fraying arms and a loose spring. She had no idea how many hours or days had passed when she awoke to the unmistakable sound of footsteps above.

Babs heard it, too. "His parents aren't supposed to be back from holiday yet," she said, meeting Caitlyn's eyes. Caitlyn rose to call for help. Babs somehow appeared at her side and slapped a hand over her mouth in what seemed like a split second, but it didn't matter.

Someone was already unlocking the door.

thirty-five

. . .

Caitlyn didn't know who or what she expected to descend the staircase: Elliot, Leanne, the police…but it definitely wasn't that guy.

"Agent Buzzcut?" Caitlyn's eyes widened. "That was you at the club that night, wasn't it?"

His lips twitched at the nickname, but he nodded.

"Wow…and you've been hanging around ever since. Wish you'd been there when Elliot attacked me. Oh man. I bet Anne Marie wishes you'd been there for her, but I guess that was my bad, wasn't it?" She considered her role in Anne Marie's present state, accidental or not, and forced a shaky smile. "All's well that ends well…sorta." Caitlyn could only imagine what he thought of her, but once it opened, she had a hard time controlling what came out of her mouth.

Agent Buzzcut wasn't looking at Caitlyn anymore. Instead, his eyes settled on Babs, who crouched in a corner of the basement, mewling in fear and desperation. Anne Marie took no interest in any of it, still asleep with one hand hanging off the side of the mattress. Caitlyn supposed the actress had no reason to fear monsters under the bed if she had already been sharing it with one.

"What's going to happen to her?" Caitlyn's gaze had returned to

Babs. "Leanne only wanted to keep her sister close, I think. There's nothing more important than the bonds of sisterhood. That's what I've heard, anyway. I wouldn't know. I'm an only child."

Agent Buzzcut raised an eyebrow as he turned to stare at Caitlyn. "I thought your kind needed more air," he said. "Have you even taken a breath since I arrived?" He turned back to Babs. "I promise the Lady means you no harm. She has someplace else in mind for you and your sister. I think you'll find the arrangement quite generous under the circumstances."

"So, this Lady…she like the H.B.I.C. of your world?" Agent Buzzcut shot another bewildered look in Caitlyn's direction. "Head bitch in charge," she explained. "It's not the nicest title, I suppose."

"You are so odd," he said, shaking his head in wonder. "There is a van outside. We will drop you and the other woman off near the hospital. Tell them…tell them you found her in the park during one of your walks. I very much doubt they'll suspect you of anything." Something in his delivery implied this was not a credit to Caitlyn's character.

"I could totally be a criminal mastermind," Caitlyn mumbled to herself as she walked across the basement to the bed. She placed her hand on the sleeping woman's shoulder. "Wake up, Anne Marie. Time to go home."

Tyler looked up as the door opened. He launched himself off the couch, pulling Caitlyn into a tight hug. He stepped back to look at her when she squeaked in pain. "Sorry," she told him. "I guess I'm a little more banged up than I thought. Don't suppose you'd be willing to scrounge up some food while I take a shower?" She turned to Max as he rose from the chair. "How much time we got until call?"

"Not much," Max said, "but are you sure you're up for it?"

"Yeah," Caitlyn touched her forehead, wincing. "They insisted on doing a brain scan when I took Anne Marie to the emergency room. No internal hemorrhaging, but I am *not* looking forward to talking to my dad when he gets the bill. I'm just glad they didn't think my head injury coinciding with her reappearance made me look suspicious."

"Did you say Anne Marie?" Tyler's eyes widened.

"Yeah, Agent Buzzcut didn't know Elliot had her, but he wasn't surprised."

"Baker." Tyler and Caitlyn looked at Max. "He introduced himself as Agent Baker."

Caitlyn appeared sheepish as she untangled herself from Tyler. "You know, it was all so hectic, we really didn't have time for small talk." She walked into the bathroom and shut the door. A grin spread across Tyler's face.

"What?"

"I dunno about you," Tyler said, "but I can't wait to see Elliot's face when she walks in."

"One thing's for sure," said Max. "It'll be one hell of a show."

thirty-six

· · ·

"The girls keep asking about her, especially the brides. Airbrushing and worry lines don't mix," Caitlyn heard Candy telling Elliot as she stepped into the hall. Tyler and Max followed behind, presenting a unified front.

"Caitlyn is no longer in the production," Elliot said.

"Gosh, Elliot, why not?" Caitlyn asked.

Elliot looked away from Candy, his eyes widening.

Caitlyn realized she held the power when she met his stricken gaze. She was all wide-eyed innocence as she gave the horrified director her sweetest smile and said, "I know you're a stickler for being on time, Elliot, but I had to help a mutual friend of ours to the hospital. Some crazy person had her locked in his parents' basement. Can you believe it?"

Candy swept past Elliot before he could answer. She peered at Caitlyn's brow. "That's quite the goose egg, pretty lady. Did you take a tumble during the power outage? No matter. We'll get you all fixed up in no time." She took Caitlyn's arm and led her to the dressing room.

Elliot's jaw tightened. Then he strode past Max and Tyler without acknowledging their existence. They smiled and gave Caitlyn a thumbs up before turning to follow. Whatever else happened, she felt at ease knowing her friends had her back.

"Cate, you're here!" Laurel's eyes widened.

"I'm sorry," Caitlyn said as she walked into the room. "I hit my head and went straight to urgent care." She decided not to reveal the truth under present circumstances. They didn't have that kind of time, and she didn't want to distract from anyone's performance.

"We were worried." Emma frowned.

"I wasn't." Everyone turned to stare at Sophia. "What? It's nothing personal."

"I should have had Max or Tyler let you know I was okay," Caitlyn said to her friends, ignoring Sophia. "After all the chaos and everything, we just didn't think…"

"Well, no more disappearing on us," Jennifer said. "Cass was so scared for you."

"I was scared for me," Amelia said with a playful grin. "I thought I was going to be stuck crawling onto the stage after all."

"Y'all. It's opening night." Hailey's eyes sparkled with excitement as she twirled in her pale pink ballroom gown. "We made it."

Even Elise smiled at that.

Caitlyn sat in a chair for hair and makeup to do their thing while the conversation moved on from her disappearance to opening night jitters. She didn't feel nervous at all. Performing for an audience was nothing compared to being trapped in a basement with creepy Babs and delirious Anne Marie. She was in her element now.

A half hour to *places*, Caitlyn knocked on the door to Leanne's dressing room. Leanne looked relieved and worried and scared all at the same time as she ushered Caitlyn into the room, casting furtive glances down either side of the hall.

"Agent Buzz, Bacon…?" Caitlyn struggled to remember his name. "Oh, whatever. Your, uhm, people…they found us. No harm will come to your sister. I think they're going to find some place…quieter, for the both of you. Safer."

"I'm not sure any place is safe for her," Leanne said sadly.

Or from *her*. Caitlyn offered Leanne an encouraging smile anyway. "Anne Marie is at the hospital now. She's going to be okay…ish." Her smile faded. "I didn't tell them what really happened. That agent thought it might leave the authorities with more questions than answers, and I guess that's not a chance your people can take. She won't remember any of it."

"What about Elliot?"

"I don't know. It's not like he can say anything without incriminating himself, and he's lost whatever hold he has on you." It didn't seem right for Elliot to go unpunished, but that sure tracked with reality as she knew it. Caitlyn pushed aside her resentment. "Someone will be waiting to take you home after the show. After that…" She shrugged.

"I'm glad you're okay." Leanne still looked sad and more than a little worried, but she smiled wanly. "I hope Anne Marie will be, too."

"They're out for blood, I just know it," Jordan told an amused Steven backstage after they snuck a peek through the curtains. Full house. *Yikes.*

"The only vampires you have to worry about are getting into costume as we speak," Steven said, giving her arms a gentle squeeze as he looked into her eyes. "It's an audience. They want to be entertained. And, okay, yeah—they probably want to say they were here if anything crazy happens—but that don't mean they're gonna bring the crazy themselves."

"You're probably right," Jordan said. She gazed at Steven, looking debonair in his elegant suit for the ballroom scene, a nice change from the tank tops and track pants he favored. Not that she ever minded seeing his muscular arms. "Break a leg. Just not, you know, for real."

Steven gave her a quick kiss before letting go of her arms. "Relax," he said. "Everything will be just fine."

As Jordan watched him walk away, she felt wound up for entirely different reasons.

Luis looked up from the prop table and grinned at Jordan.

"Not one word," she told him.

thirty-seven

. . .

After the last of the evening's audience filtered into the Blackstone Theater, Tyler started an atmospheric soundscape to set the tone before the real show began. Soft piano, leaves rustled by the wind, hooting owls, and other ambient noises. "That's the last patron," he heard Manny say in his headset. "Five minutes to showtime."

Max lowered the house lights.

Even in the control booth, Tyler could feel the audience's hushed anticipation. He felt a little anxious himself. Less about tonight's performance, more about what was to come later. How could Elliot face anyone now that Caitlyn's reappearance threatened to bring his darkest secrets to light?

Manny knew something was up, but neither Tyler nor Max could tell him the reason for Elliot's foul—well, fouler—mood. Kidnapping was a felony, but they couldn't even go to the police.

"Places," came Jordan's voice.

Tyler pushed down his trepidation. Right now, he needed to focus on the task at hand, for Caitlyn if nothing else. In her own accidental haphazard way, she had rescued the proverbial princess and defeated the bad guy—sort of. It was time for her happy ending…and new, better beginnings.

"Curtains."

Tyler brought down the music and started a prerecorded track of Michael's narration as Jonathon, setting the scene for his fateful stay in Dracula's Castle. The live orchestra in the pit began playing a haunting melody. Tyler switched on a distant wolf howl. Max brought up the lights to draw attention to key locations on the minimalist set.

"So far so good," Max said.

Tyler realized it was the first he'd spoken in a long time. "Smooth sailing, right?"

"We'll see."

If the applause they heard through the speakers in the dressing room served as any indication, the audience loved Andre. But Michael won them over with his own pretty voice and handsome face, more than holding his own against the more seasoned Broadway star. Caitlyn exchanged excited smiles with Emma and Amelia in the dressing room. "Break legs," she told the other women as they filtered out in their gowns for the ballroom scene.

Laurel reached for Caitlyn's hand on her way out.

Caitlyn gave it a squeeze. "You'll do great," she told her.

"Honestly, after telling my parents about our plans—not asking, telling—I'm not even nervous," Laurel said. "My dad is scarier than an audience of the world's meanest theater critics, and this audience doesn't sound mean at all. They want to love us. We got this." She grinned as brightly as Caitlyn had ever seen.

Caitlyn couldn't get over her own good fortune. Even twelve hours ago, she wouldn't have believed it. After all, twelve hours ago she was still stuck with Leanne's creepy life-sucking sister in Elliot's basement. *What a day. What a* life. "Everything's going so well," she gushed to Amelia and Emma.

"Too well," Amelia said.

Caitlyn noticed the other actress was fiddling with the necklace she pulled from the bodice of her costume, the cross on a beaded chain. "Are you okay?"

"Don't get stage fright on us now, girl," Emma said, grabbing Amelia's shoulders. "We're on in less than ten."

Amelia gave her a shaky grin. "I'm fine. Worried, but fine."

———

"I'm not worried," Jordan said for what felt like the umpteenth time into her headset. If it wasn't techies stumbling over set pieces, it was complaints about strange scratching noises in the orchestra pit. Onstage, everything flowed seamlessly. The audience was oblivious to any technical difficulties behind the scenes.

All eyes were on Maya.

And Maya dazzled as Lucy, belting out her bombastic number with aplomb as she shimmied and twirled from one suitor to the next. Jordan did not know if the show was Broadway-bound, but Maya sure was. These were the moments that made all the stress and heartache worth it.

Even Leanne's Mina seemed to shine brighter than usual. Jordan supposed all the speculation she had overheard was correct. Leanne simply needed the rush of an audience to come alive on stage.

And yet Jordan sensed a strange undercurrent of dark anticipation she fought to ignore. Was that a flicker of unease on Leanne's face when she glanced in Jordan's direction?

The moment faded as Leanne was transferred to the arms of another partner, her cheeks once again flushed with excitement and delight. The unsettling feeling was all but forgotten by the time the scene ended to thunderous applause. Jordan closed the curtains while the crew reset the stage for another scene at Dracula's castle.

Wolves howled as the curtains reopened. Andre spoke the words that segued into "The Children of the Night." Amelia and Emma emerged from the shadows behind Andre, but Tyler only had eyes for Caitlyn as she leapt and twirled across the stage. Max watched him with an amused smirk.

"You know, the song grows on you after a while," Tyler said, his ears red.

"Uh huh." Max looked at the stage as the three girls danced with Andre and each other. A flicker of movement in the back corner of the stage caught his attention. "Hey, did you see that?"

Tyler squinted in the direction he pointed. "I hope the song didn't attract any real children of the night," he said. He gasped and almost fell out of his chair when he saw not one but two glowing pairs of eyes upstage.

"Jordan? You seeing this?" Max asked into his headset.

"Seeing wha—Amari, no!"

thirty-eight

. . .

Caitlyn didn't know what was happening. One moment, Andre was twirling her into his arms. The next he was pushing her away and shouting as a huge creature leapt onto the stage from the shadows, landing with a thump. Caitlyn fell to the floor and watched in horror as the wide jaws of the massive dog-like beast opened. The audience gasped. Someone even whooped and cheered.

When Amari ran on stage with a heavy flashlight and struck the soul eater in the temple before it could attack Andre, the audience figured out it wasn't part of the show. Now people screamed and rose to flee as more monsters, not soul eaters, but smaller black catlike creatures with the same eerie green glow —the soul thieves Leanne had warned them about—fell from the catwalks. Caitlyn heard screams from the orchestra pit as still more creatures, even smaller than the soul thieves, poured out and into the audience. These appeared more ratlike and no less menacing than the larger beasts.

She saw Manny kicking monsters away as he tried to help people evacuate. Max and Tyler, too. Caitlyn felt a pang of affection as Tyler cast a desperate look in her direction before guiding an elderly couple out of the theater.

As people left in droves, Elliot stood motionless in the front row. His eyes fell on Caitlyn and his lips parted in the most hateful of sneers. One of the soul eaters launched itself off the stage into the audience, knocking Elliot to the ground. She heard the most awful sounds as he howled in pain. Then something more guttural filled the air, followed only by the sound of chewing.

Musicians emerged from the pit looking ragged and terrified but otherwise whole. The violinists held bows dripping with ichor of unknown origin, and other musicians used their own instruments as weapons. One carried his oboe over his head as he approached the soul eater consuming Elliot's remains. As it raised its bloodied maw, another musician dragged the oboist away.

On stage, Luis, wielding a prop sword, threw one to Andre. Caitlyn rose from the floor and ran to the prop table, grabbing one for herself. She swung it at the soul thieves and smaller unknown monsters that had Amelia and Emma cornered.

Jordan was on the phone with 911. "I said what I said, lady. Can you hear the commotion? Send help!"

———

After Max and Tyler helped Manny and the ushers guide people outside to safety, where a growing crowd had gathered on the sidewalks, Tyler turned to go back inside. "You can't go back in there," Manny said.

"Yeah, you're not stopping him." Max patted Manny on the back before following Tyler in.

"Wait, who are you?" Max heard Manny ask, but he didn't turn to see who the general manager was talking to.

Inside, the theater was emptier but no less quiet as the battle continued onstage. The actors and crew on stage huddled together as monsters surrounded them. Several pairs of eyes turned to glare at Max and Tyler, the largest belonging to the soul eater who now slouched toward them from the front row, blood and flesh falling from its gaping maw.

"You weren't kidding about the vicious raccoons," Max said. His laugh sounded high- pitched and maniacal even to himself.

"We are so fu—" Tyler started to say, but a familiar voice echoed off the walls as it chanted. The beast whimpered and lowered its head. Other monsters mewled in anger and disappointment as men and women in black suits walked down the main aisles, speaking in that same unfamiliar tongue as the first. Each held a wicked blade carved in an ornate pattern with colorful jewels in the hilt.

Agent Baker and his fantastic fairy friends had arrived.

Max sat down right there on the floor, shaking his head. "This is bullshit," he said.

———

Onstage, the monsters slunk away and disappeared into whatever shadows they'd come from as half a dozen men and women followed Caitlyn's dear old friend with the buzzcut into the theater. One appeared to tear a hole into the fabric of reality itself with their dagger, ushering the smaller ratlike monsters through the opening. Caitlyn turned away for sanity's sake. Too weird. Even after everything that had happened. Some questions were better left unanswered.

Emma and Amelia hugged her and each other. Their hair fell in tangles and their costumes clung to their damp skin, but they appeared unharmed. Jordan's brother Amari looked shell shocked as he clung to his sister, resting his head on top of hers as they sat huddled in a corner. Andre and Luis shook hands and clapped each other on the back, looking tired and sweaty but remarkably unfazed.

Caitlyn turned to stare out into the auditorium. She had words for Agent Bacon Bits, but that could wait.

Tyler turned as Caitlyn ran down the steps and into the audience. She threw herself at him and planted a noisy kiss on his lips. "Not my best work," she said with a wild smile, "but it'll have to do for a start." Tyler felt his ears and cheeks grow warm as he stared at her. Then, he pulled her close for a second attempt.

Someone cleared his throat as he approached the trio. Caitlyn pulled away from Tyler to glare at Agent Baker, hands on her hips. "Friends of yours?" She gestured at the last of the little beasties as his people drove them back into whatever hell dimension they came from.

"Not exactly," he said.

"Well, this is going to be one hell of a public relations nightmare for you," Max said as he pushed himself to his feet.

"You don't know the half of it," Agent Baker said. "But you'll be amazed at how little we have to suggest for people to rewrite their own versions of these events to serve their vision of reality." He walked away, to help speed the process along, Tyler assumed.

"Not that amazed." Caitlyn sighed before turning to Max and Tyler. "We need to check on the rest of the cast and crew." Tyler followed Caitlyn and Max followed him. Jordan and the rest had already left the stage.

Caitlyn stepped through the door and walked past the dressing rooms. Lloyd of all people comforted a crying but unharmed Maya in hers. Johan stood nearby, clutching a bloodied hand to his chest while talking to a concerned Andre and Jordan.

"This one thought the ladies needed his help, and we barely pulled him back into the room in time," Christopher said, indicating with his shoulder as he leaned against the doorway of the men's dressing room.

Nicholas sat in a chair whimpering as Matthew tended to his wounds with cotton balls and rubbing alcohol. "You might want to consider getting a rabies series," he said.

"Seven days," one of the others teased in a creepy voice.

Poor Nick. At least he might get his chance to apologize to Anne Marie. Caitlyn pursed her lips. He didn't actually want that chance, did he?

The door to the women's dressing room opened and Leanne walked out. She nodded at Caitlyn. Laurel followed behind her. "The others keep thanking her for being so brave and for checking in on us, but she did so much more than that," Laurel whispered to Caitlyn.

Telling themselves stories to explain the weirdness away already…

…It's probably for the best, Caitlyn decided.

———

Tyler stood outside and watched as paramedics loaded Nicholas and Johan onto ambulances, with Nicholas doomed to get the first of several rabies shots just in case. Johan had already gotten a preemptive vaccination for fear of rabid dogs. Big Stephen King fan, that one. He thought there was no greater threat in the States, except for maybe killer clowns and malevolent teenagers.

It was Amelia who asked the question everyone was thinking once the police were done taking wildly varying witness reports from the cast and crew. "What happens now?"

Caitlyn turned to Tyler with sad eyes. He pulled her into his arms and held her close.

"I said you were welcome to stay with us as long as you needed," Max told Caitlyn. "And the offer still stands." He smiled. "Even if you two insist on making it weird." He appeared to consider making it a group hug, but laughed and folded his arms across his chest instead.

thirty-nine

. . .

Opening night of Elliot Dunn's ill-fated **Dracula** *musical began and ended perhaps the only way it could have, with a surprise evacuation after a pack of wild dogs infiltrated the Blackstone Theater one week ago today. Apart from the shocking death of the director himself, only minor injuries were reported, but the pack of wild dogs remains at large with sightings reported everywhere from Central Park to the sandy beaches of Long Island.*

While Animal Control and the NYPD have few answers, the show, it so happens, will go on. The Lafayette Foundation, a private organization which has its fingerprints on everything from the arts to education and healthcare, has stepped in to assume financial control of **Dracula.** *Sources confirm Andre Petrov remains in the titular role, with rising star Maya Jackson as Lucy. The stress of the production proved to be too much for newcomer Leanne Snow, who has been replaced in the role of Mina by Amelia Lopez.*

Dates have been set for a new opening in late July. Tickets are selling fast.

"Are you disappointed?"

Caitlyn looked up from the newspaper article to raise an eyebrow at Max. "About Amelia? Are you kidding? I love her. And she and

Michael make a great pair. If he wasn't gay, I'd 'ship them. I'm just glad this Moira Lafayette, whoever that is, wants the show to continue without any further recasting."

"I can't believe Anne Marie was willing to come back, and to a smaller role," Tyler said. "She really doesn't remember anything that happened?"

"No," Caitlyn said. "She really doesn't. I think she's just happy to be alive, to be honest."

"And I'm happy you don't have to move back home," Tyler said.

"I should finish packing, though." Caitlyn gestured at her duffel bag. "I'm supposed to meet everyone at the apartment in an hour. Then Cass is taking me thrifting. I guess she finds my minimalist approach to decorating as distressing as my wardrobe." She leaned in to kiss Tyler and laughed when it made his ears turn as red as the first time.

Max rolled his eyes. "Why do I have a feeling I'm still going to be tucking the two of you in every other weekend?"

"You weren't even home until five this morning. We heard you sneaking around, trying to be all stealthy. Doesn't work when you're bumping into everything."

Caitlyn smiled as Max and Tyler continued to banter back and forth like an old married couple. She had friends, a home, a boyfriend, a steady gig. Sure, the world might be descending into otherworldly chaos, and she'd forever wonder if a soul eater or who knew what else was lurking around the next corner, but for now, things were looking up.

acknowledgments

Thank you to my husband, Michael.

Thank you to Cari Dubiel, Kaytalin Platt, and G.A. Finocchiaro at Writing Bloc for all you do.

Thank you to Mom, Dad, Karen, Susan K Hamilton, Carolyn Markowski, and Dan Keleher for your ongoing encouragement.

Thank you to Lock City Books for the local support and your cat adoption services (which really has nothing to do with me or my books, but makes me happy just the same).

Thank you to our own cats (and rats) for the company, but not the unsolicited editsasfdagdfzuhjgf.

And a big thank you to you, the reader.

about the writing bloc

The Writing Bloc is a writing group and independent publisher. We help writers reach their writing goals, and publish books by passionate authors. We're a working collaborative writing community—a place to work together on everything from beta reading to marketing.

We publish short story collections, anthologies, mysteries and thrillers, science fiction, horror, fantasy, and contemporary romances produced by our members.

Find us at:
writingbloc.com
Twitter: @writingblocpub
Instagram: @writingblocpub
Facebook: /writingbloc
Facebook Group: facebook.com/groups/writingblocgroup

9 798986 554389